HARVEY ANGELL

HARVEY ANGELL

Diana Hendry

RED FOX

HARVEY ANGELL
A RED FOX BOOK 978 1 849 41656 6

First published in Great Britain in 1991 by Julia McRae,
an imprint of Random House Children's Publishers UK
A Random House Group Company

First Red Fox edition published 1993
Reissued 2003
This edition published 2012

1 3 5 7 9 10 8 6 4 2

The Random House Group Limited supports the Forest Stewardship Council (FSC®),
the leading international forest certification organization. Our books carrying the FSC
label are printed on FSC®-certified paper. FSC is the only forest certification scheme
endorsed by the leading environmental organizations, including Greenpeace. Our paper
procurement policy can be found at www.randomhouse.co.uk/environment.

MIX
Paper from
responsible sources
FSC® C016897

Set in 13.5/17.5pt Bembo by Falcon Oast Graphic Ltd.

RANDOM HOUSE CHILDREN'S PUBLISHERS UK
61–63 Uxbridge Road, London W5 5SA

www.randomhouse.co.uk
www.kidsatrandomhouse.co.uk
www.totallyrandombooks.co.uk

Addresses for companies within The Random House Group Limited
can be found at: www.randomhouse.co.uk/offices.htm

THE RANDOM HOUSE GROUP Limited Reg. No. 954009

A CIP catalogue record for this book is available from the British Library.

Printed and bound by CPI Group (UK) Ltd, Croydon, CR0 4YY

Contents

Diana Hendry has published more than forty books for children and teenagers. She won a Whitbread Award for *Harvey Angell* and a Scottish Arts Council Book Award for *Harvey Angell Beats Time*. Two of her picture books, *The Very Noisy Night* and *The Very Snowy Christmas*, have been adapted for the stage by Blunderbus Theatre Company. Diana has published four collections of poetry for adults and one for children. She's a frequent tutor on creative writing courses at the Arvon Foundation. She's worked as a journalist, an English teacher and a university tutor and for a year was writer-in-residence at a hospital. She lives in Edinburgh.

For Hamish – with love

You think, when you plug your hoover in, that you are buying electricity from the Electricity Board. Actually you are using energy from the sun.

Richard Gregory

CHAPTER 1

Henry saw the sign on his way home from school and at once his heart sank to his sandals. The sign said ROOM TO LET. The words were printed in big black and white letters and attached to a stake. It looked as if someone – Aunt Agatha – had stabbed the stake into the front lawn as into the heart of an enemy. As a result, the house itself looked angry, ashamed of its empty room and embarrassed that everyone should know about it in this way.

Not that 131 Ballantyre Road ever looked exactly happy. It was a tall narrow old house with a roof that frowned over the top windows. It was heavily – and dirtily – curtained (Ballantyre

Road was on the main bus route into the city) and if you looked carefully you could see bolts and locks everywhere. No one had painted it for years and no one had done anything to the garden. The only cheerful thing about the garden was a straggly line of very tall purple and pink hollyhocks.

When he first came into the house, when he was taken over by Aunt Agatha after the death of his parents, Henry had been cheered by the hollyhocks. He had decided they were a laughing kind of flower. They seemed to be saying, 'We don't care about the roar of the traffic. We don't care that no one looks after the garden. We don't care that there isn't much sun. We can grow and flower and laugh all by ourselves.' And that's what they did. Now and again Aunt Agatha threatened to cut them down as if all that laughing offended her and gave her house a frivolous look. But she never did. She stomped past them on her way to the shops and the hollyhocks waved and nodded at her, but Aunt Agatha refused to give them the time of day.

The sign ROOM TO LET was set in a clear space

just to the left of the hollyhocks. Henry could easily guess which room had, overnight, become empty. The attic.

The attic was a difficult room to let. Most of it was taken up with a sloping ceiling that came down from the roof to the floor. It was more like half a pyramid than a proper room, and into this space Aunt Agatha had squeezed a bed, a shelf, a rack for clothes, a table just about large enough for a mug and a plate and – for the last six months – Mr Murgatroyd.

Mr Murgatroyd was one of Aunt Agatha's mistakes. He was over 1.67 metres and plump. Aunt Agatha did not like her lodgers to be either too high or too wide. Height and width suggested large breakfasts to Aunt Agatha and no one was given a large breakfast at 131 Ballantyre Road. They were given thin slices of toast (not more than two per person) and a cup (not more than one) of weak tea. Sometimes there was a scraping of marmalade to go with the toast, but most often it was just toast and margarine. Aunt Agatha didn't approve of sugar either and always told her lodgers she was looking after their teeth and that's why there wasn't any.

Aunt Agatha had broken her rules about height and width because Mr Murgatroyd was a baker at the bread shop round the corner. He baked loaves which Henry thought had wonderful names like Granary and Harvester and Bloomer and each night he brought one home and gave it to Aunt Agatha. This was a Great Saving on breakfasts and Aunt Agatha liked nothing more than a Great Saving.

But Mr Murgatroyd got plumper and plumper (and perhaps taller, too) on his Granaries and Harvesters and Bloomers. He kept knocking over the table in his attic room and banging his head on the ceiling. This happened particularly in the middle of the night. Mr Murgatroyd was an adventurous dreamer. Often his dreams were so exciting that he would sit bolt upright in the middle of them – and then *bang*, he would crack his head on the ceiling and all the other lodgers lay very still and quiet (but wide awake) while Mr Murgatroyd said very rude things to the ceiling.

It is possible that all those bangs on the head

in the middle of the night did something awful to Mr Murgatroyd's brains. There had been a terrible row between him and Aunt Agatha. Henry, huddled on the bed in his own small and dark basement room, had listened in and had been surprised that Mr Murgatroyd, usually a quiet man, could think of so many rude things to say, even though he had had practice shouting at the ceiling.

'You're a penny-pinching skinflint!' shouted Mr Murgatroyd. 'You're a mean and miserly money-grubber! You're a stingy, scrimping Scrooge!' said Mr Murgatroyd. 'And if you think I'm going to pay you a penny of rent you can think again. Look at these bruises on my head! *You* should be paying *me* to sleep in that – that postage stamp you call a room.' (Henry could almost see Aunt Agatha turning pale at the idea of her paying Mr Murgatroyd.)

Finally Mr Murgatroyd had thrown a Bloomer at Aunt Agatha, which bounced off her bony shoulder and broke on the floor. Henry knew this because, when he dared to come out of his room, he found Aunt Agatha sticking the loaf together again and they all ate it the next morning at breakfast – except Mr Murgatroyd, who wasn't to be seen.

Henry didn't hurry when he saw the sign in the garden. Whenever a lodger left like this, in a hurry, it meant that there was an empty room in the house that *wasn't earning money!* This was terribly painful to Aunt Agatha. Henry knew that they would all be down to one piece of toast for breakfast, and that until they found a new lodger he would lie in bed at night unable to sleep while Aunt Agatha groaned over her accounts and her rent books.

The truth was that the only person who could have fitted fairly easily into the attic was Henry himself. He was still just about small enough. He had often hoped, as lodger after lodger left to look for something better, that his aunt would give him the attic room. His own room in the basement was no bigger but a great shrub in front of the window blocked out all the light. It was difficult to read by his 15 watt light bulb – Aunt Agatha was as mean about electricity as she was about breakfasts – and the floor was damp.

There were great holes under the skirting boards and a variety of beetles and spiders swept in with the draught. Henry had grown quite fond of them. All the same he would happily have given them up for the attic room.

If he was in the attic, Henry thought, able to look out high over the roofs of the city, to see the zips of light up the sides of offices at night, to see where the churches stood proud in the daytime – why, then he would be like the hollyhocks, growing and flowering and laughing all by himself. Sometimes, down in the dark damp basement, Henry thought he might shrivel up altogether like an unwatered, unsunned plant. (There were many of these in the back garden.)

But there was no hope at all that his aunt would give him the attic room. Not when she could charge £50 a week for the privilege of banging your head on the ceiling.

Nor was there any hope that the attic would be taken by anyone young and cheerful, anyone that might be a friend to Henry. Mr Murgatroyd had been the best they'd had at Ballantyre Road for a long time. Often he'd slip Henry a crumpled croissant or a sticky piece of Lardy cake, or a little twisted plait of bread.

But Mr Murgatroyd had been a 'mistake' as far as Aunt Agatha was concerned and she would be very careful to stick to her rules and not make another.

Lodgers at 131 Ballantyre Road should not be more than 1.6 metres tall and 126 pounds (preferably less) in weight. They should not be too healthy, too cheerful or too young. All these qualities suggested An Appetite – for life and for breakfast that Aunt Agatha disapproved of. Aunt Agatha didn't like anyone who talked too much (they might argue about the rent) and she was very careful not to take in anyone who played a musical instrument.

Aunt Agatha couldn't abide music. Once she had caught Henry listening to a violinist on the radio. 'Music weakens the moral fibres,' said Aunt Agatha, snapping off the radio. And that was that. Henry didn't know much about his moral fibres but he liked music. He was glad that morning assembly at school included songs.

Henry's favourite daydream was that he

belonged to the school orchestra. He imagined himself looking very solemn and grand with a cello, or being the boy who clashed the cymbals at the exciting moment, or even conductor of the orchestra. But it was only a dream. Aunt Agatha would never let him play an instrument. Probably she thought that even a triangle would weaken his 'moral fibres' – whatever they were.

There was a very old piano in the kitchen. Someone, long ago, must have played it, but Aunt Agatha kept it firmly locked and the key hidden. Henry had often searched for the key but had never been able to find it.

Henry trudged the last few yards to the gate of 131 and nodded at the hollyhocks as cheerfully as he could. They were jiggling about today as if they'd heard something very funny or someone had tickled them under their leaves.

Henry went down the basement steps, un-locked the double lock on the door and went in. There were voices in the kitchen and another sign on the door knob said 'Interviewing'.

Henry knew his aunt well. She would have spent all day questioning people in search of somewhere to live, turning away everyone jolly, everyone lively, everyone young, looking for someone who would match the other tenants, someone pale, frail and frightened; someone who would never dare chat to Henry, someone like Miss Muggins (first floor right) who sometimes whispered 'hello' to him and then scuttled away.

Trying to think of the joke the hollyhocks had been laughing at, Henry went into the kitchen.

CHAPTER 2

Aunt Agatha, like her house, was tall, old and narrow. On a good day, when she swept her hair up into swirls (like the ice cream in an ice-cream cornet) and put on her best dress, she could look quite elegant. On a bad day, like today, she looked taller, older and narrower than ever before. Sometimes Henry looked at the photographs of Aunt Agatha that stood on top of the piano in their tarnished silver frames and wondered what had happened to her. Here she was as a bride, all plump and pretty and smiling. And here she was with a baby in her arms looking gentle and happy.

Henry had never seen Aunt Agatha looking

either. He thought that somehow or other Aunt Agatha had wintered. The plumpness, the prettiness, the gentleness and happiness had dropped off her like leaves at the end of summer and left her gaunt and stark as a winter tree.

Henry knew at once that Aunt Agatha had had a bad day because of the angry angle of the pencil she kept behind her ear to do her accounts. It looked more like an arrow than a pencil. Aunt Agatha sat at the kitchen table with her sharp eyes and pointed nose directed at a large cheery-faced man with ginger whiskers, a tartan waistcoat and a black beret.

1.8 metres at least, thought Henry, and not a hope of fitting into the attic.

Ginger-Whiskers was smiling hopefully at Aunt Agatha. Aunt Agatha looked as grim as a funeral.

'Tell me something about your diet,' said Aunt Agatha. Ginger-Whiskers looked cheerier than ever. He grinned at Henry.

'Well now, Miss Agatha, I'm pleased to tell you that I've a very healthy appetite and that I'm not a fussy man. No, not me. I'll eat anything I'm given.'

Which wouldn't be very much, thought Henry.

'I see,' said Aunt Agatha frostily. She pulled the pencil out from behind her ear. Henry, standing behind her, saw her write down 'Greedy'. He could also see that there were a long list of names in Aunt Agatha's notebook, all of them crossed out and given a final judgement like 'too tall', 'too fat', 'too talkative', 'too cheerful'.

'Henry!' said Aunt Agatha, turning sharply. 'You can start peeling potatoes for supper.'

Henry dumped his bag in the corner and went over to the sink. Ginger-Whiskers gave him a wink. Henry tried to wink back although winking wasn't yet one of his talents. Whistling, yes. Winking, no. Now if Ginger-Whiskers should move in . . .

Aunt Agatha carried on with her questions. She reminded Henry of detectives he'd seen on television questioning criminals. He dug in the potato bag under the sink and counted out five potatoes (one each) and found the knife. If Aunt Agatha *was* a detective she'd be saying, 'Now tell me the truth. You do like eggs for breakfast, don't you? You've been lying to me. You're really a cereal–bacon–and–egg man. You probably have two cups of tea, you nasty little creep.'

'Your personal habits now,' Aunt Agatha was saying. 'Baths and so forth.'

'Oh, I'm very clean, ma'am,' said Ginger-Whiskers eagerly, bowing slightly, as if, Henry thought, Aunt Agatha was the Queen. 'I bath every morning and then I do my exercises. I keep myself clean and healthy.' Ginger-Whiskers took a couple of deep breaths and puffed out his chest to prove his health and strength. Aunt Agatha winced.

'A bath every morning,' she repeated as if totting up seven baths at ten pence a bath.

'That's right, ma'am!' said Ginger-Whiskers.

Henry giggled. Aunt Agatha turned on him. 'Watch what you're doing, Henry!' she snapped. 'Peel those potatoes properly. And keep the peelings. Waste not want not.'

This was one of Aunt Agatha's favourite sayings and it had taken Henry quite a long time to decide that it was quite untrue. At 131 Ballantyre Road they wasted nothing and wanted a lot.

'You have a regular job?' inquired Aunt Agatha.

'Oh yes, ma'am,' said Ginger-Whiskers proudly. 'I play in an orchestra. I play the trombone.'

Aunt Agatha snapped shut her notebook. Henry ran the cold tap loudly to hide his giggles. Aunt Agatha stood up and folded the frosty boughs of her arms across her chest. Henry imagined Aunt Agatha in a judge's wig, about to give sentence.

'I'm afraid, Mr, er – Mr, er . . .'

'Mr Cannon,' prompted Ginger-Whiskers.

'Oh yes . . . Cannon,' said Aunt Agatha, frowning as if even his name was too loud for her delicate hearing. 'Well, I'm afraid, Mr Cannon, that I really don't think you would be suitable for our little community of residents. I make it a rule, you see, no musicians. We lead a very quiet life here. I'm afraid it would be far too disturbing to have you and your drums . . .'

'Trombone,' said Ginger-Whiskers, 'it's the trombone I play, and of course I keep the mute in it when I'm practising.'

'Nevertheless . . .' said Aunt Agatha and moved to the door.

Henry knew that 'nevertheless' was almost always Aunt Agatha's final word on a subject. Ginger-Whiskers looked as if he was about to protest. He turned red and then white, opened his mouth and closed it and then marched angrily out of the door that Aunt Agatha held open for him.

When he was safely on the other side of it, he put his mouth to the letter-box and shouted, 'Nevertheless – I'm glad I'm not living here!'

'Common!' said Aunt Agatha. 'Common and vulgar! I've wasted the whole day on common and vulgar folk who I will not – are you listening, Henry – not have in my house. And hurry up with those potatoes!'

She swept out of the kitchen. Henry sighed and put the potatoes in a pan. There were so many things that were common and vulgar to Aunt Agatha. Eating was one of them. So was music, it seemed. Particularly if played on a trombone.

Henry set the pan on the cooker and tried winking with first his left and then his right eye, but they both kept going together. He didn't dare whistle in the house. Aunt Agatha thought whistling was *very* vulgar. Whistling was a kind of music.

Supper that night was even more miserable than usual. Promptly at six o'clock Aunt Agatha banged the gong in the hall and all the lodgers came hurrying downstairs. If you were late, Aunt Agatha was likely to say, 'Not very hungry tonight?' and give you a smaller helping than usual.

They all had their places at the table. Aunt Agatha sat at the top and Henry at the bottom with the four lodgers in between them. Tonight there was Mr Murgatroyd's empty chair. An empty, non-paying chair. And no bread. No one dared mention Mr Murgatroyd's name, but the row of the night before, his absence now, and the lack of bread made him more present than if he had really been with them.

Miss Muggins sat on the right of Aunt Agatha. Miss Muggins moved about the house like a little ghost. Henry thought she was probably about seventy. She worked in the newsagent's down the road and was just about tall enough to see over the counter. She was so thin and had such a poor appetite that she had actually been known to leave a quarter of a potato on her plate. And at once, Mr Murgatroyd reached over and finished it off for her. Aunt Agatha had said nothing. She had just arched her eyebrows and looked and Mr Murgatroyd and everyone round the table knew what that look said. It said, 'Vulgar! Common and vulgar!' No one had ever dared do that again although once Henry had caught Aunt Agatha finishing off two sprigs of cauliflower left by Miss Muggins.

Miss Skivvy sat next to Henry. Henry guessed that if Miss Muggins was seventy then Miss Skivvy was seventy-five. Miss Skivvy was also thin. Had she stood up straight she would have been taller than Miss Muggins, but long years working in the post office and bowing to Aunt Agatha had made her permanently bent. Henry liked Miss Skivvy. Once she had given him some first day covers and sometimes, when Aunt Agatha was out shopping, Miss Skivvy would nudge Henry in the ribs with a bony elbow and say, 'Let's have a cup of tea, shall we?' And they would hurry into the kitchen. They never used Aunt Agatha's tea because she counted her tea bags every night. But Miss Skivvy had her own supply and sometimes produced ginger biscuits. On one such occasion Miss Skivvy had told Henry how she had come from the country to look for the man of her dreams but he had never arrived and somehow she had got stuck here, waiting.

Miss Skivvy always said, 'Good Morning' to the hollyhocks and Henry thought she probably still missed the country and the man of her dreams because sometimes he woke to hear her crying in the night.

Mr Perkins, at sixty, was the youngest lodger. Mr Perkins worked in the bank. Henry thought there couldn't be much work for Mr Perkins in the bank because Mr Perkins seemed to spend so much time in the library, and sometimes Henry saw him sitting in a café near the school, reading again and making a cup of tea last a very long time.

Still, Mr Perkins went out every morning sharp at eight-forty-five carrying a briefcase and a rolled up umbrella. And sometimes at supper, when the silence was simply so enormous that Henry thought he might drown in it, Mr Perkins would sigh noisily and say, 'Very busy at the bank today. So many customers!' And Aunt Agatha would say, 'Indeed, Mr Perkins! Too much easy money around. It's all get up and grab these days. Waste not want not, that's what I say.'

And Miss Muggins and Miss Skivvy would nod their heads in agreement.

It was always Mr Perkins too who was prepared to ask a question that no one else dared to ask. Tonight Mr Perkins considered the table, then his plate on which lay such a thin slice of ham that you could see the plate's pattern through it, the one potato peeled by Henry and a teaspoon of peas.

'No bread tonight, I see,' said Mr Perkins a little mournfully. 'And no Mr Murgatroyd.'

'Mr Murgatroyd has had to leave us,' said Aunt Agatha.

Miss Muggins gasped. She had not heard the row. She thought that one more blow to Mr Murgatroyd's balding head had been fatal.

'Not . . . not *dead*?' she whispered.

'No one dies here!' snapped Aunt Agatha, as though dying, like eating, was vulgar and common.

'No, no! Of course not. I quite forgot,' said Miss Muggins.

'No, he has simply gone elsewhere,' said Aunt Agatha.

'Pity,' said Mr Perkins.

(Yes, thought Henry, catching Mr Perkins' eye and wondering if he too was thinking Granaries, Harvesters, Bloomers.)

Aunt Agatha seemed to read their minds. 'I think not,' she said. 'Too much starch really isn't good for you, Mr Perkins. I have noticed that you'd got a little portly lately. Maybe you should cut out potatoes?'

'Maybe I should cut out conversation,' said Mr Perkins crossly.

Aunt Agatha pretended to titter at this. 'Conversation never made anyone fat, Mr Perkins. Nevertheless . . .'

Oh dear, thought Henry, no potato for Mr Perkins tomorrow night. 'And have we found a new tenant for that charming room upstairs?'

asked Mr Perkins. 'Someone to join us in our happy home?'

'No one suitable has applied for the vacancy,' said Aunt Agatha.

Henry could have sworn Mr Perkins said something like, 'No one fool enough!' But if he did, he did it under the clatter of dishes being cleared away.

The remark, said or unsaid, echoed in Henry's head that night when he lay in his own room trying to read with a small torch Miss Muggins had given him one Christmas. Mr Perkins was right, no one would be fool enough to live here unless, like Henry, they had to.

Henry shone his torch on the few things in the room he could call his own. Once upon a time, before the accident in which his parents had died, there had been a great many things. Henry could remember a large house full of sunshine, chatter, laughter and – though he couldn't be certain – Henry had a memory of music. His mother singing and his father joining in. There had been friendly furniture, coloured tablecloths, flowery curtains, brightly woven rugs, lamps that made patterns on the wall. Aunt Agatha had sold them all.

'Your parents have left me a little money,' she said, when she came to collect him from the far north of Scotland. 'But a very little. Not nearly enough for your keep. All this will have to go.' And go it did. Henry's bed had been kept, a little iron bed his mother had painted red and a small wooden chair and chest of drawers. There was also a painting that Aunt Agatha had been on the point of selling only Henry had sobbed and shrieked so loudly that the man buying the rest of the furniture had said, 'Oh, let the lad keep that. It's not worth much.' And Aunt Agatha, who at the time had been trying to look as sweet and kind as an aunt should look, had agreed. It was a painting of a doorway looking into a house that was all warm and cosy and inviting.

Sometimes Henry sent himself to sleep imagining he was walking through that doorway. But tonight it was difficult to get to sleep. The dark shrub outside rustled against his window. Beyond were the hollyhocks, nodding in the moonlight. Thinking up a new joke for the morning, perhaps. But next door, in the kitchen, Henry could hear Aunt Agatha counting her tea bags.

Tomorrow there would probably be more criminal investigations of would-be lodgers and some new and no doubt ancient person would join them. And there'd be no more Granaries, Harvesters or Bloomers. Very soon, thought Henry, he'd be as skinny as Miss Muggins.

CHAPTER 3

Mr Murgatroyd was missed even more at breakfast time when, as Henry had guessed, they were down to one piece of toast each.

Aunt Agatha was clearly still in a bad mood. She looked almost grey, as if, Henry thought, she'd been up all night counting the tea bags and the rents and now had tea bags under her eyes.

Aunt Agatha slammed the kettle on the hob as if daring anyone to protest about the toast. No one did. Even the brave Mr Perkins said nothing although he did hold his slice of toast up to the light and then shake his head.

Henry wished *he* was braver. He wished he could say, loudly and cheerfully, 'Can I have another piece of toast, Aunt Ag?' the way he'd once heard Jem Croker say to his mum. Jem Croker's mum had answered, 'Yes, of course, dear. One slice or two?'

Henry knew that not in a million years would Aunt Agatha say that. Sometimes Henry imagined scenes in which he stood on the kitchen table and Aunt Agatha cowered beneath him while he demanded a great feast. 'I want chicken and chips, followed by lamb and roast potatoes, followed by apple crumble and cream, followed by strawberries and ice cream, followed by lemonade and six bars of chocolate,' he would command from the imaginary heights of the table. And Aunt Agatha would scurry about saying, 'Yes dear, right away dear, three bags full dear.'

Or he would lead a protest march down the street. Henry had seen one about pensions, so he knew what to do. He and Mr Murgatroyd would carry a big banner that read BIGGER BREAKFASTS AT BALLANTYRE ROAD! and DOWN WITH RENTS! UP WITH TOAST!

Henry knew he could do neither of these things. He knew that Aunt Agatha only had to arch her eyebrows and wither him with a look. It was the withering Henry couldn't stand. It made his stomach shrink, his heart shrink, even his hair . . . It was as if something wintery in Aunt Agatha struck out at him and made him shrink under the soil like plants do at the onset of frost, not to reappear again until spring. There was the same wintery feeling about the house. A dead feeling about it as if there was no corner in which a boy might play.

Semi-shrivelled (just at the thought of the wintery withers) and very empty on one slice of toast, Henry collected his books and went off to school.

It was sunny but windy. The hollyhocks were as tall as the first floor windows now. They tossed and rocked in the wind as if they were having hysterics. 'You'd better be careful,' Henry warned them, 'or you might laugh your heads off.' But the hollyhocks only tossed some more as if they'd never heard anything so silly.

Henry wished the baker's was open. He might call in and see Mr Murgatroyd and Mr Murgatroyd might slip him a still warm bun.

But it was too early. Henry hadn't realised how dependent he'd become on Mr Murgatroyd's Harvesters, Granaries and Bloomers or considered how he'd get by without them. He felt hungry everywhere.

At that time, Henry didn't know just how hungry he was. He was too busy thinking about food to know that his eyes were hungry for green trees and his ears were hungry for music and his heart was hungry for a friend. Henry didn't know all this because he was busy thinking about school lunch.

His class was at first sitting today. That meant twelve-fifteen. Henry was glad. He didn't think he could have made it until second sitting at one-thirty. Almost everyone else said school dinners were deadly. All stodge, they said. Lumpy potatoes and concrete jam sponge. But Henry was glad to get some lumps and concrete inside him. He ate everyone else's left-overs and was very glad Aunt Agatha wasn't there to arch her eyebrows and say, 'Common, Henry! Vulgar!'

Walking home from school, quite nicely weighted inside, Henry thought he might survive quite well, Mondays to Fridays. It would be weekends and holidays that were difficult and the holidays — all six weeks of them — were horribly near.

The wind had blown itself out during the morning. Now it was hot with the dry, dusty hotness of the city. Turning into Ballantyre Road, Henry saw at once that the sign was down. He began to hurry, trying to push down the absurd hope that someone young and happy and summery had taken the attic room.

The hollyhocks were perfectly still now. They stood with their flowery heads lifted as if listening in to something, as if they had heard some amazingly good news and were struck still with astonishment.

Henry went into the kitchen trying to steel himself for another Miss Muggins or Miss Skivvy, someone about eighty who wouldn't say boo to a goose and certainly not to Aunt Agatha.

There at the kitchen table sat Aunt Agatha, *smiling,* and drinking tea with a stranger.

CHAPTER 4

The stranger was a small, neat man. He had soft fair hair the colour of thatch, a rather long nose and eyes that might have been green and might have been blue and might have been grey. All you could truly say about them was that they were changeable. He wore denim dungarees – brightly patched at the knees – and carried a canvas tool bag.

A builder, or a plumber, thought Henry. Aunt Agatha has at last decided to have the leaks in the roof mended.

While Aunt Agatha sat at the table drinking her tea and *still smiling*, the stranger, cup in hand, wandered curiously about the kitchen, peering into things and under things and – yes, surely he was sniffing!

The gas man, thought Henry. Aunt Agatha might not mind about water leaking in, but she *would* mind a gas leak. That was it. The stranger was the gas man.

'Henry,' said Aunt Agatha, 'I want you to meet our new lodger, Mr Harvey Angell.'

Henry's mouth fell open. Harvey Angell turned and beamed at Henry. He had a very infectious beam. Without thinking about it, Henry beamed back. Then he did think about it and carried on beaming because there was nothing frail or frightened about Harvey Angell. Small and skinny as he was, he was undoubtedly both healthy and happy.

'So this is Henry,' said Harvey Angell. 'I'm very glad to meet you, Henry. I don't like to live in a house where there isn't a child. No connections, you see.'

Henry didn't see but he felt too shy to say so. Harvey Angell was wandering about the kitchen sniffing again. 'Plenty of connections here,' he said happily.

Henry looked about him as if trying to see the kitchen with Harvey Angell's eyes. It was a big room. There were, he noticed for the first time, quite a lot of electric sockets. One for the cooker, one for the kettle, one for the electric fire (although Aunt Agatha only used this when it was minus ten), one for the iron and two spare.

'Mr Angell is a kind of electrician,' said Aunt Agatha.

'Researching Energy Fields,' said Harvey Angell, turning at least a 500 kilowatt beam onto Henry. Aunt Agatha looked suitably impressed by this high-sounding phrase.

'You can start scraping the carrots, Henry,' she said. 'Mr Angell and I have just a few more details to sort out.'

Henry went and fetched the carrots. They were the old gnarled ones that the greengrocer sold off cheaply. He picked out the five largest and put them in the colander.

'As you've seen,' said Aunt Agatha, 'the attic room is very – er – very compact. Everything to hand, you might say.'

(You might indeed, thought Henry. You might even say everything to foot, seeing as you could reach everything by not stirring one.)

'It's perfect,' said Harvey Angell. 'I shall be busy with my research and, being small – being, well, compact . . .' Here Harvey Angell laughed, a bright youthful laugh such as hadn't been heard at 131 Ballantyre Road for at least ten years. The window panes – only just hanging in their rotten frames – rattled with alarm. Aunt Agatha gave them a look and they stopped.

'Your age again, Mr Angell?' queried Aunt Agatha.

'Twenty-nine going on ninety,' said Harvey Angell smoothly.

I must be hearing things, thought Henry, and indeed Aunt Agatha only seemed to have heard the first part of Mr Angell's reply because she said, 'Ah yes, twenty-nine – rather young for this establishment, I'm afraid, Mr Angell. In this household we are all very quiet. Very quiet indeed. I trust your research won't be noisy?'

'Not at all, not at all . . .' said Harvey Angell. (He was sniffing, Henry was sure of it now, actually sniffing at the dresser, opening a cupboard door and sniffing inside it.)

'My research,' said Harvey Angell, 'is so quiet it's almost ghostly!' And he laughed again.

Henry wished he wouldn't. Laughter made Aunt Agatha grate her teeth. She could still change her mind, and although Henry felt very uncertain about all that sniffing, he desperately wanted Harvey Angell to stay.

'And you don't eat breakfast?' said Aunt Agatha.

'Never!' said Harvey Angell. 'I'm out and about in the Energy Fields early in the morning. Catching the vibes, you know. No time for breakfast. Oh, and because I'm up early in the morning I like to be in bed early.'

Aunt Agatha smiled.

It was beginning to make sense, thought Henry. Aunt Agatha had found someone small enough to fit the attic, someone who didn't eat breakfast, someone who went to bed early and who therefore – even if he was researching electrical energy, whatever that was – wouldn't be using much of the actual metered, expensive kind.

Harvey Angell's sins of youth and cheerfulness could be forgiven him and a week or two at 131 Ballantyre Road would probably cure him of his laughter. But what on earth were the Energy Fields that Harvey Angell was up and about in, early in the morning? Henry tried to imagine fields all growing crops of little brown, green and blue wires like you got in the inside of plugs, all trembling with their vibes early in the morning.

'Well, that's settled then,' said Aunt Agatha. 'The rent will be £50 a week, payable on a Monday morning by ten o'clock.'

'A very old dresser, this,' said Harvey Angell, bending down to sniff along the edge of it.

'It was my grandmother's,' said Aunt Agatha.

Henry was surprised. Somehow he had never thought of Aunt Agatha as having a grandmother, or a mother for that matter.

'Quite warm,' said Harvey Angell, patting the dresser. 'A good Energy Field, that.'

What on earth did the man mean, wondered Henry, dropping the carrots in the pan.

'Do another one for Mr Angell,' instructed

Aunt Agatha as if she'd counted the plops.

'Would you like some rent in advance?' asked Harvey Angell, turning away from the dresser and giving Aunt Agatha The Beam.

Henry thought Aunt Agatha was going to faint or cry. She took off her spectacles and wiped her eyes.

'Well, that would be very pleasing, Mr Angell,' she said. 'Very pleasing. Now, do you have some luggage?'

'This is it,' said Harvey Angell, indicating the canvas tool bag.

'How wise of you,' said Aunt Agatha. 'Too many possessions weigh a man down, clutter the place up.'

Henry thought this was a great cheek on Aunt Agatha's part. 131 Ballantyre Road was full of clutter. Weighed down with it. None of it new, of course, and none of it very clean. It occurred to Henry, for the first time, that it must once have been both new and clean. He began to think about Aunt Agatha's grandmother and with a sudden surprise realised that whoever she was, she would have been his great-grandmother.

'Henry will take you up to the attic,' said Aunt Agatha. 'Supper is at six sharp. You'll hear the gong.'

Henry picked up the tool bag. Harvey Angell took three ten pound notes out of his back pocket and gave them to Aunt Agatha.

While he waited, Henry patted the dresser as Harvey Angell had done. It wasn't at all warm. It was decidedly cold.

CHAPTER 5

'Well now, isn't this fine?' said Harvey Angell when they reached the attic.

'It's very small,' said Henry apologetically. 'Mr Murgatroyd kept banging his head on the ceiling.'

'Murgatroyd?' repeated Harvey Angell quickly, sniffing the air as if for some lingering aroma of Harvester, Granary or Bloomer. 'Murgatroyd? Murgatroyd? Ah yes! I've got him. The baker!'

'That's right!' said Henry, surprised. 'Do you know him?'

'I wouldn't say I *know* him,' said Harvey Angell, dumping his tool bag on the bed (the mattress immediately sank an inch), 'but I've got a lot of connections . . .'

'You do have a very nice view up here,' said Henry, opening the window. 'You can see the wedding cake church from here. I call it that because it goes up in tiers. And most of the offices stay lit up at night. They make patterns in the dark. It's nice.'

'Terrible waste of electricity,' said Harvey Angell. He did not seem at all interested in the view. When Henry looked round, Harvey Angell was down on his knees sniffing under the bed.

'Is it all right?' asked Henry anxiously. 'I don't think there are any mice. But I suppose there might be. Mr Murgatroyd often brought a loaf up to bed with him.'

'No. No mice,' said Harvey Angell, getting up briskly and dusting his patched knees. 'Daisies. Definitely daisies.'

'I didn't think daisies had a smell,' said Henry, feeling that this was a very silly conversation.

'You have to have a nose for them,' said Harvey Angell, 'if you're a Transmitter, that is.'

There is something very wrong with my

ears, thought Henry. Had the new lodger said 'transmitter'? He must have said 'electrician' and whatever it was that was wrong with Henry's ears had changed it into 'transmitter'. But why should an electrician need a nose for daisies? He was about to ask this, but Harvey Angell had opened up the tool bag.

'Come on, help me unpack'

Henry helped. He tried, at the same time, to have a quietly polite and experimental sniff or two (Aunt Agatha always said sniffing was vulgar. 'Use your handkerchief, Henry!' she would cry). But he could smell nothing.

The unpacking didn't take long. Harvey Angell had two pairs of dungarees and two shirts (they hung them on the clothes rail); and one pair of very heavy boots. For the Energy Fields, thought Henry. But as if reading his thoughts, Harvey Angell said, 'Those are to keep me earthed! Now, here's the important stuff. All my Connecting Kit.'

Henry shivered a little, he didn't know why. It was as if he'd had a very small electric shock. What was it Aunt Agatha said when she shivered like that? 'Someone walked over my grave', that was it. Harvey Angell smiled at him and instantly Henry felt warm and comfortable again.

The only electrician Henry had ever seen had been the one who sometimes came to school to put in extra plug sockets. Henry had not paid much attention to the man's tools but he had a faint memory of screwdrivers, coils of coloured wire, thin silver bands of fuse wire on a card, a torch, a pair of pliers. Harvey Angell's Connecting Kit was nothing like this.

'We'll put everything on that shelf,' said Harvey. 'Be very careful.'

Henry nodded.

'Screwdrivers,' said Harvey Angell, passing Henry a bundle of them. They were of all sizes and had bright plastic handles.

'Energy Charger,' said Harvey, handing Henry a small machine with a range of numbers in a semi-circle and a red needle.

'And my Best Beloved,' said Harvey Angell, and he pulled a silver flute out of his bag.

'Aunt Agatha won't allow that,' said Henry at once. 'She hates music. It's a wonder she didn't check up on you.'

'A wonder, eh?' said Harvey Angell, polishing the flute on his bottom.

'Yes,' said Henry. 'No one who plays music is allowed a room here. Aunt Agatha says music weakens your moral fibres.'

'Strengthens the connections,' said Harvey Angell, briskly tucking the flute under his pillow and turning back to his bag.

'Maybe your Aunt Agatha needs oiling. Music is the oil of life.'

Henry giggled.

'Now, last but not least . . .' said Harvey Angell, and he pulled from his bag a large, carefully wrapped package. When he unwrapped it Henry saw that it was a clock. The face of the clock was so covered in flowers and animals that you could hardly see the numbers and the fingers were as fine and silvery as fuse wire. Perhaps they *were* fuse wire?

This is all very odd, thought Henry. What if Harvey Angell was not an electrician at all, but some kind of master criminal or a spy – hiding out in a small attic in Ballantyre Road because no one would think of looking for him there?

Harvey had taken a screwdriver and was busy attaching a plug to the clock's wire. He was very neat and deft at it. Henry felt a bit better.

'Watts and volts, watts and volts,' sang Harvey Angell. 'Better by far than thunderbolts!' And he smiled at Henry.

The smile was irresistible. Henry found himself thinking that he didn't care if Harvey Angell *was* a master criminal or a spy. He liked him. He liked him more than anyone he had ever met before.

All the same, there was Aunt Agatha to think about. Henry could not truly say that he was fond of Aunt Agatha, but he wished her no harm. And there was Miss Muggins and Miss Skivvy and Mr Perkins to think about. They were all people who needed looking after.

'You go along now,' said Harvey, 'before your aunt bangs that gong of hers and wakens the dead. I'll be down in a volt or two.'

His ears again, thought Henry. What Harvey *must* have said, or *meant* to say, was 'I'll be down in a minute or two'.

Thoughtfully, Henry went down into the kitchen. Aunt Agatha was laying the table. She was not smiling any more but she was no longer cross. There was not an empty, unpaid for room any more. There was not an empty, unpaid for chair at the supper table.

'Get the plates out, Henry,' said Aunt Agatha. 'You shouldn't need telling. And fill the jug with water, too.'

Henry did as he was told.

'Aunt Agatha,' he began, not quite knowing how he was going to ask what he wanted to ask, 'Aunt Agatha – do you think – do you think Mr Angell's all right?'

'All right? What on earth do you mean?' asked Aunt Agatha, slapping down a small pudding spoon in each place (a small spoon made your pudding look bigger). 'I think he's very all right. A week's rent in advance and very polite. Oh yes, very polite. Not a greedy man. Doesn't have a vulgar appetite. Mr Perkins could take a tip or two from Mr Angell.'

'But do you think he's a proper electrician?' persisted Henry.

'A proper electrician?' echoed Aunt Agatha. 'Henry, what is the matter with you today? Of course he's a proper electrician. You saw his tool bag, didn't you? And anyway, I've got references.'

Henry did not want to start talking about the strange items in Harvey Angell's tool bag – particularly the clock and the flute. After all, he could be quite wrong. There was no point in worrying Aunt Agatha and also, Henry realised, he was dying to find out more about Harvey Angell.

'What did the references say?' he asked.

Aunt Agatha put the salt and pepper pots on the table. 'I think you've been watching too much television, Henry,' she said. 'There're the references – on the dresser. See for yourself.'

Henry went over to the dresser and picked up the letters. They were both very brief. The first said:

Dear Sir or Madam,

I am very happy to give Mr. H. Angell this reference. He made all the connections in our house and since then they have been in perfect working order.

Yours faithfully,

The second letter, when Henry unfolded it, was even briefer. It said:

TO WHOM IT MAY CONCERN
I wish to commend to you Mr Harvey Angell.
He works with great energy.

That was all. Henry was about to fold this up again when he noticed the date at the top, 7th May, 1891.

The same shiver, the 'someone's-walking-over-my-grave' shiver went over Henry, but he said nothing. It was probably a slip of the pen. Someone had obviously *meant* to write 1991, not 1891. It was easily done.

A very little voice inside Henry's head said, 'Yes, and what about those other slips? The ones you've been hearing? Like, "You need a good nose to be a Transmitter". And, "I'll be down in a volt".'

Henry shook his head.

'Henry, you have filled that jug three times and emptied it three times,' said Aunt Agatha. 'Please concentrate on what you're doing.'

'Connections,' said Henry. 'I'm trying to make connections.'

'I should like you to connect the water with the jug,' said Aunt Agatha.

'Aunt Agatha, who was your grandmother – the one who owned this dresser – my great-grandmother? What was her name?'

'Good gracious, child! Surely you know the name of your own great-grandmother. It was Ellen, of course. Grandma Ellie we called her. Your mother must have talked about her?'

'I don't remember,' said Henry. 'She spoke of a grandma, but I don't remember a name. And maybe there were Christmas presents from her . . . but she seemed so old and so far away that – well, she didn't seem quite real.'

'She was very real indeed!' said Aunt Agatha. 'She spent all her life in this house. Born here, married here, died here.' Aunt Agatha sighed.

Henry looked about him. Until now all the old and broken-down furniture in the house had seemed anonymous, belonging to no one. He'd never thought about things like the dresser and how things could be hundreds of years older than he was. At least, he hadn't thought about it until Harvey Angell had arrived and had come sniffing around things. Henry looked at the corner cupboard with its brass knob that needed a screw fitting to hold it properly in place. He looked at the funny scrolly wooden chairs at the table. He looked at the locked up piano with its curly candlestick holders, one on either side. And he thought, Great-Grandma Ellie, *my* Great-Grandma Ellie, has probably touched everything in this room. Things haven't been cleaned in here for so long that if I was a detective I bet I could still find her fingerprints! He got The Shiver again, just thinking about it.

Aunt Agatha had sat down, the knives and forks still in her hand like a bouquet of spiky metal flowers. 'She should have sold it, this house,' she said. 'Or I should have sold it. Once upon a time it was a happy house. Then . . . then it became an unhappy house.'

Henry set the jug of water down on the draining board and sat down at the table with Aunt Agatha.

There were just the two of them in the big,

usually gloomy kitchen. They had never sat down together like this. Henry noticed that the late afternoon sun had caught the pattern from the old (and dirty) lace curtain and printed it, in silhouette, on the floor. For a moment the kitchen felt suddenly cosy.

'Tell me,' he said, 'why it was a happy house and how it turned into an unhappy house.'

'There were three things your Great-Grandma Ellie never got over,' said Aunt Agatha. 'One of them was your mother's death. Your mother, Lizzie, was her favourite grandchild. Of course she loved us both, Lizzie and me. She brought us up, you know, when our mother went off . . .'

'Went off?' echoed Henry. 'Your mother went off and left you?'

'Upped and offed, never to be seen again,' said Aunt Agatha.

Henry sat back in his chair. He suddenly felt rather cross with Aunt Agatha. Henry liked to think that he was the only person in the world whose mother had gone off. Everyone he knew, everyone at school, had a mother. Mothers, as far as he knew, stayed put. Except, until now, his own. He wasn't sure that he wanted to share a lost mother with Aunt Agatha. To himself, Henry didn't think, 'My mother is dead,' or, 'My mother has gone to heaven,' (which is what people told him). No. Henry thought, 'My mother has gone off and left me,' and secretly he felt very angry about it.

It had to be secretly because you could not very well say to someone else – to anyone else in fact – 'My mother has gone off to heaven without me. Isn't she mean?' It would sound very silly. People would laugh. Worse still, Henry thought it was probably wicked too.

He remembered how, after the accident, the vicar had come to call. He had put his arm round Henry's shoulders and said, 'God must have wanted your mother at his home in heaven.' And Henry had pulled away from the vicar and run into the garden screaming at the top of his voice. He could hear himself screaming now. Screams that you would have thought would have pierced the sky and got right through to his mother wherever she was. Only they hadn't.

Henry blushed when he thought about this.

But the truth was that he still felt much the same way now as he had then, only he didn't go round screaming, of course. Why should God want his mother more than he, Henry, did? God had plenty of mothers up there in heaven. Why Henry's? And although he knew it wasn't her fault, that she hadn't meant to leave him when she'd gone out that night in her best summer dress promising to bring him back something special, he couldn't help blaming her a little. Sometimes at night, looking at the painting of the doorway into the warmly inviting house, Henry found himself saying to his mother (as if she could hear him), 'Why weren't you more careful?' or, 'Why didn't you tell me you were going forever?'

'Did she die then, your mother? Do you mean she upped and offed and died?' Henry asked.

'Good heavens, no!' said Aunt Agatha. 'It was after the war, you see. Father – your grandfather – was killed in action. We had a telegram telling us. Mother couldn't manage without him. She was very young and a party girl. She got very lonely all by herself and not having much money to look after us with.

'One day we came home from school, Lizzie and I, and there she was all dressed up in her one and only party dress. She was wearing very long white gloves. Funny that, me remembering those gloves. They were so long and special – so white – I felt she didn't want to touch me in them. Anyway, there she was in her party frock and a hat – oh, brimming with life, that hat – flowers and birds and I don't know what. And she said, "I'm off for a little holiday, girls. You're going to Grandma Ellie's." There was a taxi waiting for her at the gate . . .'

'And you never saw her again?' asked Henry.

'I tell a lie,' said Aunt Agatha. 'We saw her once more. She came back to visit us here. She was very brown and she wore a gold necklace and a gold bracelet. I remember how they shone against her skin. She looked very healthy and happy and we all felt very pale and . . .' Aunt Agatha's voice tailed away.

'Unhappy,' said Henry.

'Yes,' said Aunt Agatha. 'Unhappy.'

'Weren't you angry with her? Her leaving you like that?' he asked.

Aunt Agatha gave Henry a long, considering kind of look. Then she leant across the table and patted his hand. 'Very,' she said. 'If you really want to know, I was spitting mad! Lizzie and I went down to the bottom of the garden and jumped up and down with rage. I remember Lizzie always said that jumping up and down did you a power of good.'

Henry laughed and Aunt Agatha laughed in return.

'But then, you see, Grandma Ellie looked after us,' continued Aunt Agatha. 'That was when this house was a happy house. Grandma Ellie liked to watch Lizzie painting. They'd both go up to the attic, Lizzie would paint the view from the window. I'd be down here . . .' Aunt Agatha broke off and her face, which memories had made gentle, grew severe again. 'But things didn't turn out like that. When Lizzie died – well, it was just too much for Grandma Ellie. She died only days afterwards. There'd been the other sorrows, you see. Her own daughter, my mother, upping and offing and then . . . after that . . . after that . . .' Aunt Agatha's voice seemed to vanish backwards into time and then return, sharply, to the present. 'Look at the time, Henry! It's half-past six. The potatoes will be ruined.'

'You can't stop there!' cried Henry desperately. 'What happened? What was the second thing?'

'It's got nothing to do with you, Henry,' said Aunt Agatha, getting up from the table. 'Nothing at all.'

Aunt Agatha marched out into the hall and banged the supper gong so loudly that the plates shook on the dresser.

Henry set them straight again. They were not just any old plates, they were Great-Grandma Ellie's plates, and whatever had happened to make Great-Grandma Ellie stop painting and to make Aunt Agatha lock herself up in winter just as surely as the piano was locked up *did* have something to do with him. He was sure of it.

CHAPTER 6

Supper with Harvey Angell at the table was very different from any supper Henry had known at 131 Ballantyre Road. To begin with, Harvey Angell was very complimentary about Aunt Agatha's cooking.

'What deliciously tender chicken,' he said, quickly eating the fragment on his plate. 'I'll have another helping of that if you don't mind, Miss Agatha.'

There was a hush at the table. Everyone waited for Aunt Agatha's eyebrows to arch and for her familiar speech about controlling the appetite. But it seemed Aunt Agatha didn't mind. She went over to the oven and fetched the pot. Mr Perkins, Miss Muggins, Miss Skivvy and Henry all stared in astonishment, their knives and forks poised in midair, as Aunt Agatha gave Harvey Angell a second – and really quite generous – portion of chicken.

'Well, if there're seconds going . . .' said Mr Perkins cheerfully.

'There aren't,' said Aunt Agatha, clamping the lid back on the pot. 'Mr Angell doesn't eat breakfast. Nor, if I might remark, does he have any excess weight about his person.'

Mr Perkins glowered. Harvey Angell leant across the table to Miss Muggins.

'Forgive my asking, Miss Muggins,' he said, giving her the irresistible 500 kilowatt beam, 'but was it you I heard singing in the room beneath mine this evening?'

Miss Muggins became very red and tearful. 'I'm most terribly sorry, Mr Angell,' she said, giving a frightened glance at Aunt Agatha. 'It was such a nice evening that I couldn't resist singing to myself. I was trying to do it as quietly as I could. I'm most sorry if I disturbed you. Most sorry indeed. I do assure you it won't happen again.'

'Nothing to be sorry about,' said Harvey Angell. 'I enjoyed listening.'

Miss Muggins was thoroughly flustered by this. 'Oh, how very kind,' she kept saying until Mr Perkins, still cross that he hadn't been allowed second helpings, slammed down his knife and fork, saying, 'Fine words butter no parsnips.'

'I beg your pardon, Mr Perkins,' said Miss Muggins. 'We don't have any parsnips, do we?'

Mr Perkins groaned.

'Nothing makes a place more like home than a little music, a song or two,' continued Harvey Angell, 'and I see we have a piano over there.'

The cheek of this stranger was all too much for Mr Perkins. 'It's locked!' he shouted, pushing his chair away from the table, standing up and waving his pudding spoon at Harvey Angell. 'It's locked like everything else in this house. Locked up like the fridge at night. Locked up like the tea bags. Locked up like laughter, like love ... like ... like Hearts in Unkind Bosoms!' finished Mr Perkins and with something almost like a sob he left the room.

'Oh dear,' said Miss Muggins, 'did he want parsnips that badly?'

'Mr Perkins is a poet,' said Aunt Agatha calmly. 'I'm afraid he's very moody and temperamental. I do apologise on his behalf, Mr Angell.'

'Mr Perkins works in the bank,' said Henry. (He'd been on Mr Perkins' side about the second helping.)

'No,' said Aunt Agatha. 'He only *pretends* to work in a bank. I've known it for years.'

'Anyway,' she continued, 'neglect and hunger are good for poets. They write much better poems without second helpings.'

'Well, you should know about the artistic temperament, I suppose,' said Harvey Angell. 'Being a musician yourself, that is.' Henry saw that Harvey Angell was giving Aunt Agatha the Full Beam. He waited for his aunt's anger, waited for the speech about music and moral fibres.

Instead Aunt Agatha flushed scarlet and suddenly looked very shy. 'However did you know?' she asked.

'He sniffed it out,' said Henry, making a wild guess.

'Henry, don't be silly,' snapped Aunt Agatha.

'You've got pianist's hands,' said Harvey Angell.

Aunt Agatha promptly hid them under the table cloth.

'People think that pianists have long slender fingers,' said Harvey Angell, 'but you only have to look at the hands of some famous pianists to know that's not true. I've seen photographs of Anton Rubinstein's hands – stumpy little fingers he had, but a long stretchy thumb. And Franz Liszt, much the same.'

'Do show us your hands, Miss Agatha,' said Miss Skivvy and, reluctantly pleased, Aunt Agatha took her hands out from under the cloth and spread them out on the table. Everyone leaned forward to admire them. Aunt Agatha stretched her thumb out as far as it would go – which was at a right angle to her fingers. Everyone else tried to do the same and failed.

'Well, isn't this grand then,' said Harvey Angell. 'It seems we've got one singer and one pianist. We can have a sing-song.'

There was a sudden silence. This is it, thought Henry, he's gone too far this time.

'The piano *is* locked, Mr Angell,' Miss Skivvy whispered as if she was saying, 'the piano's dead', as well it might be, thought Henry, locked up and unplayed like that for years.

'Henry, the key is on the top shelf of the dresser,' said Aunt Agatha suddenly.

Henry fetched a stool and reached up for the key. He dusted it off on the back of his trousers.

'I'll just pop up for my flute, then I can join in,' said Harvey.

Henry looked to see if Aunt Agatha flinched at this clear infringement of the No Music rule, but she didn't. It was as if, Henry thought, Harvey Angell's Beam cast a kind of spell on Aunt Agatha. He thought of Ginger-Whiskers and his trombone. A pity he isn't here too, he thought, then we'd have a regular orchestra.

'What about you now, Miss Skivvy,' said Harvey Angell, pausing at the door, 'any musical accomplishments?'

'Well, I can recite,' said Miss Skivvy. 'I know *The Forsaken Merman* off by heart.' Henry had never seen Miss Skivvy so excited except during their illicit tea-making sessions.

'Splendid!' said Harvey Angell, making for the stairs. 'I'll knock on Mr Perkins' door as I go up. Perhaps he'll read us one of his poems?'

It was a wonderful evening. Afterwards Henry tried to think what had happened to Aunt Agatha and why, at the piano, she had seemed so different.

Something happened to the stiff winteriness of Aunt Agatha's body when she sat down at the piano. Maybe your Aunt Agatha needs oiling, Harvey Angell had said. Well, that was it. The music worked like oil which got inside Aunt Agatha and oiled all her bones and joints. Aunt Agatha swayed and bent to the music and sometimes even joined in the singing with Miss Muggins.

Henry had expected Miss Muggins to have a high, thin little voice – a voice that matched her size. But no! Miss Muggins had a powerfully deep voice. She sang *Land of Hope and Glory* and another song called *The Old Folks at Home* which made Miss Skivvy cry.

Mr Perkins had been persuaded to come downstairs by Harvey Angell but he still looked very cross.

'Some people have only been here five minutes and then take over the place,' he said. 'They are given quite unwarranted privileges. For myself,' said Mr Perkins, 'I do not like people who go sniffing about the place,' and he looked very pointedly at Harvey Angell.

That gave Henry a shock. In the enjoyment of the evening he had temporarily forgotten his doubts about Harvey Angell. Doubts which, it seemed, were shared by Mr Perkins.

'Mr Perkins, you're being very foolish,' said Aunt Agatha. 'You're only jealous. Have you brought a poem down?'

(Poor Mr Perkins, thought Henry, he can't charm Aunt Agatha with a Beam.) But Mr Perkins *did* have a poem. It was pages and pages long. Henry couldn't understand a word of it but it seemed to be about love.

Everyone applauded at the end except for Aunt Agatha who said, 'Reeee-asonable, Mr Perkins, but you could cut the third verse and the seventh and the tenth and it would be much better.'

Mr Perkins sat down and sulked.

'Well, I thought that was very fine,' said Harvey Angell. 'Poets are very like electricians. We're on the same circuit, you could say. Exploring the Energy Fields. There was once a very fine poet called William Blake who said, "Energy is Eternal Delight".'

'I don't know what you're talking about,' said Mr Perkins crossly. 'Poets are nothing like electricians. Nothing at all.'

But Harvey Angell only laughed at this and then it was Miss Skivvy's turn to give her recitation.

Henry liked Miss Skivvy's poem better than Mr Perkins' poem even though it was just as long and he fell asleep in the middle of it.

Miss Skivvy's poem was about a merman and his children calling for a lost mother. It was a roundabout sort of poem with lines that kept on repeating themselves like the call of the children. In Henry's sleepy brain the lines went round and round too, so that he seemed to be joining in the sadness of the forsaken merman when he sang,

Children's voices should be dear
(Call once more) to a mother's ear;
Children's voices wild with pain –
Surely she will come again!
Call her once and come away;
This way, this way!
'Mother dear, we cannot stay!
The wild white horses foam and fret.'
Margaret! Margaret!

Come, dear children, come away down;
Call no more!
One last look at the white-wall'd town,
And the little grey church on the
    windy shore;
Then come down!
She will not come though you call all day;
Come away, come away!

'A very sad poem,' said Harvey Angell when Miss Skivvy, wiping her eyes because she had been so moved by her own performance, had finished.

'Even though I'm very old,' said Miss Skivvy, 'I often miss my mother.'

'I know the feeling,' said Harvey Angell. 'A mother lost is a paradise lost. At least we think it's lost, though it's there, on the circuit, all the time.'

(Anyone would think, thought Henry, that mothers were being lost all over the place, that they were as easily lost as handkerchiefs or homework.)

'All this about circuits, all this electrical jargon,' said Mr Perkins irritably, 'I've had enough of it!'

'I think you should give us a tune, Mr Angell,' said Miss Muggins. 'Something to cheer us all up.'

So Harvey Angell played his flute and Henry felt very wide awake then because it was a very happy tune so that even Mr Perkins was soon tapping his feet to the rhythm.

Harvey Angell walked about as he played. Henry thought of how, when it was very hot in late summer, Aunt Agatha walked about the kitchen with her Death Spray, killing flies and wasps. Harvey Angell walked about with his flute in much the same way, only he was blowing music – Life Spray – into every corner.

After this Harvey Angell said he must go to bed for he had to be up early in the morning for work and everyone else discovered how late it was too.

Aunt Agatha was about to lock the piano up again when Henry said, 'Leave it open, Aunt Agatha. Please.' And Aunt Agatha gave him an odd kind of look and said, 'Well, all right Henry.'

Then to his astonishment she opened the window onto the back garden and threw the key away.

It had, he thought as he undressed for bed, been a whole day of surprises. From the moment Harvey Angell had arrived things had begun to change. And the people in the house had changed too. Or maybe, thought Henry, it wasn't that they had changed but just that he had learnt more about them. Miss Muggins, for instance, and her singing; Mr Perkins and his poems; Aunt Agatha and her mother who had upped and offed and Great-Grandma Ellie who once upon a time had seemed as unreal as a person in a book and who now, even though she was dead, seemed very real indeed.

A little parade of woodlice crossed Henry's floor. Henry knelt down to look at them. He was fond of woodlice. They looked like armoured tanks. They all looked exactly alike – although some were bigger than others – but probably, if you got to know them, they all had very different characters. 'Do you sing, Mr Woodlouse?' Henry asked the woodlouse leader. 'Or do you play the flute?' Then he laughed at himself and got into bed.

The dark bushing shrub outside his window rustled against the pane. It seemed to Henry that the shrub and the darkness had caught the echo of Miss Skivvy's poem and as he began to doze off, the lines of the poem went round and round in Henry's head:

> She will not come though you call all day;
> Come away, come away!

And then Henry was going down, down, down into the under-the-sea world of sleep.

Suddenly – at least it seemed sudden, but it must have been two or three hours later – he was wide awake again. There were footsteps on the stairs.

The stairs of 131 Ballantyre Road were very creaky. During Mr Murgatroyd's stay in the attic, Henry (sometimes wanting to creep up there to share a crust of Granary, Harvester or Bloomer) had learnt how to go up and down them avoiding the creaks.

Whoever was out there now hadn't. Henry knew the footsteps of everyone in the house, even the very light ones of Miss Muggins.

Henry slid out of bed and very quietly opened his door. Very quietly – avoiding the creaks – he crept halfway up the stairs.

In the moonlight that shone through the landing window Henry saw him, Harvey Angell, peering into the linen cupboard at the top of the stairs and – yes – sniffing!

Sniffing about! An occupation that surely belonged to thieves, criminals and kidnappers! What was Harvey Angell doing in the middle of the night sniffing about in the airing cupboard? Sniffing out treasure maybe? Did Aunt Agatha have any gold and silver? Had Great-Grandma Ellie a treasure horde? Had it all been locked up, like the piano, like – what was it Mr Perkins had said? Like Hearts in Unkind Bosoms? Gold and silver locked up in a chest somewhere?

Henry wondered if he should cough loudly or switch on the light and say casually, 'Hello there, Mr Angell. Looking for something? Can I help you?'

But the stairs and the landing with the moonlight shining down into the sleeping house seemed suddenly spooky. And what did he know about Harvey Angell? Really know? What was that song he'd sung while unpacking his Kit?

Watts and volts,
Watts and volts,
Better by far
than thunderbolts!

If he disturbed Harvey Angell now, mid-sniff as it were, he might very well turn round and throw a few watts and volts at Henry and Henry would be frizzled and fried on the instant.

He tiptoed back to bed and huddled under the blankets. Although it was a warm night, he felt The Shiver again.

But I *will* find out about him, Henry vowed to himself. I'll find out exactly what he does with that Connecting Kit of his and – and this seemed a brainwave – I'll follow him one morning to the Energy Fields.

And with this thought Henry fell asleep. He dreamt that Harvey Angell had gone down to visit the merman and his children and was fitting their underwater palace with electric lights. The Forsaken Merman was very keen to have an electric kettle because he wanted to make tea. Tea was very comforting, the merman said. So

Harvey Angell fitted an electric kettle with a piece of seaweed for the lead and the merman boiled it. But when the kettle boiled, the sea boiled too and then Aunt Agatha appeared like some ancient, sea-wrinkled queen and said he wasn't to boil that kettle ever again. It was a waste of electricity.

CHAPTER 7

When Henry woke up in the morning, Harvey Angell had already gone out.

'Up with the lark,' said Aunt Agatha. 'He drank a glass of water and was gone. Singing something about watts and volts.'

'Better by far than thunderbolts,' said Henry.

'What are you on about, Henry?' said Aunt Agatha. 'You'd do well to follow Mr Angell's example when it comes to getting up in the morning. If you don't hurry you'll be late for school.'

Aunt Agatha, it seemed, had already been following Harvey Angell's early morning example. The kitchen, Henry noticed, looked suddenly brighter and cleaner. The old lace curtains had been taken down and were blowing on the line. You could actually see through the window now and into the back garden where somewhere, among the weeds and waist-high grass, lay the key to the piano which Aunt Agatha had so grandly thrown away the night before.

'Mr Perkins has offered to do some gardening for me,' said Aunt Agatha.

'Isn't he pretending to go to the bank today?' asked Henry.

'No,' said Aunt Agatha. 'Mr Perkins has given up pretending.'

'No, I haven't,' said Mr Perkins, appearing in the kitchen. 'I've only given up pretending about some things. I like pretending. It cheers me up greatly. This morning, while I was getting dressed, I was pretending that I'd have two pieces of toast for breakfast.'

'And so you have,' said Aunt Agatha. 'If you're working in the garden you'll need plenty of energy.'

'"What is now proved was once only imagined,"'

declared Mr Perkins. 'There, that's something else that William Blake fellow said. Your Mr Angell isn't the only one who knows the great poets. I imagined a second piece of toast – and here is the proof!' Mr Perkins picked up his two pieces of toast and waved them happily in the air.

'He is not *my* Mr Angell,' said Aunt Agatha, 'and are you deliberately trying to make your toast cold, waving it about like a football rattle? *I* am going to imagine that you have eaten your breakfast very quickly and begun work in the garden. *And* I am going to pretend that Henry is on his way to school.'

Henry laughed, put his breakfast dishes in the sink and picked up his bag. It was odd, but it seemed to him that Aunt Agatha and Mr Perkins rather enjoyed arguing.

Henry felt more light-hearted this morning. It was easy, he thought, to pretend or imagine things in the middle of the night that seemed very silly the next morning. The only things that had happened since Harvey Angell's arrival had all been good things. Extra toast (there had been extra for Henry, too) was a decidedly good thing, so was an unlocked piano, so was a sing-song and clean windows and Aunt Agatha being altogether more auntly.

As Henry went out he noticed there were some new hollyhocks sprouting and that these new ones were almost white, as if the old hollyhocks had exhausted their colours and produced this new, last, snow-white child.

The snow-white hollyhocks seemed like a good omen to Henry. Everything that had happened in the last two days, including these new hollyhocks, seemed to suggest that Harvey Angell was a force for good, not evil. But then – and Henry paused, halfway down the road – that was the whole point really.

Harvey Angell did seem to possess some kind of force or special power. Somehow or other he got to work on people. It was as if, thought Henry, they were all like dead batteries before the coming of Harvey Angell, and now they were all re-charged. I'm getting carried away with all this electrical jargon, thought Henry and he hurried on to school.

But even though, in the sunshine, Henry had decided that his fears of the night before were foolish, one of the things that had been 're-charged' was his curiosity. He spent most of the day thinking about Harvey Angell's Connecting Kit and wondering if – were he to ask politely – Harvey Angell would explain it all to him.

When he got home from school the house was empty. The windows had been flung wide open and the hollyhocks were nodding and peering inside. The hall floor had been polished and Henry saw, for the first time, that it was not the dull grey he had presumed it to be, but that it was made of a neat pattern of red and black tiles.

Henry went into the kitchen and looked out into the back garden. No sign of Mr Perkins, but lots of evidence of Mr Perkins' hard working day. Two large flower beds had been weeded and half the lawn scythed and mowed. The lawn mower stood in the middle as if Mr Perkins had just popped out. Probably to the library, thought Henry. Never a day went by when Mr Perkins didn't go to the library.

Aunt Agatha's shopping basket wasn't on its usual hook either. Henry remembered that it was Friday, the day when Aunt Agatha 'stocked up', as she called it, although stocking up to Aunt Agatha meant buying just-about-enough flour and just-about-enough tea and just about-enough potatoes. And no more than just-enough.

All was silent upstairs too. Clearly neither Miss Muggins nor Miss Skivvy were home from work yet. And Harvey Angell? Was he somewhere in the house? Sniffing about maybe?

It was then that Henry decided to do some sniffing about himself. His curiosity about the Connecting Kit had, during the day, become like a terrible itch or a ravenous hunger. To think of the Connecting Kit up there in the attic was like knowing there was a wonderful chocolate cake sitting in a tin on a shelf just above your head.

Henry almost ran up the stairs. Of course he would knock and see if Harvey Angell was in and then he would make his polite request to be shown the Kit. I could say that I've decided that I want to be an electrician, thought Henry. And it wouldn't be a lie, just a kind of pretend, like Mr Perkins' pretend about the bank. But if he's not in . . . well . . . someone has to look after Aunt Agatha, Henry told himself.

There was no answer to Henry's knock. Excitement and fright made Henry's hands all clammy and wet. He opened the door and went in.

The attic looked much as it had when he had helped Harvey Angell to unpack. Henry went straight to the shelf. He was hoping that Harvey had not taken the Connecting Kit with him. What a relief! He hadn't!

It was all there on the shelf. But now that he looked at the various items, they all seemed very dull. The screwdrivers were perfectly ordinary screwdrivers. There was nothing hidden among the handkerchiefs. The Energy Charger, Henry presumed, as a way of testing either batteries or electrical appliances. Anyway, he had nothing to test it on. There was no flute. For reasons beyond Henry's understanding, Harvey Angell obviously needed his flute when he was out in the Energy Fields.

He was just resolving never to be stupid again when he heard it. The clock's tick.

The clock did not tick the way a normal clock ticks. Henry sat very still and listened. No, the clock did not have a regular tick. Nor a regular tock. In fact it was a very jumpy clock. Henry began counting the ticks. First the clock did ten very rapid ticks, then there was such a long silence Henry thought it had stopped forever. Then it began again, but more slowly this time, and now it gave out eight rather slow tocks. Yes, definitely tocks. A most musical clock, thought Henry! It went back to the beginning again, hurrying along now with ten – no, twelve quick ticks, then silence again.

Harvey Angell had put the clock on the small ledge by his bed. Henry knelt on the bed to look at it more carefully.

It was a very hard clock to tell the time by. This was Henry's first thought because the face of the clock was so covered with paintings of flowers and animals you could hardly see the numbers and the fuse-wire fingers were so thin you could hardly see where they pointed.

But when he had stared at the clock for the length of ten quick ticks and eight slow tocks,

Henry began to be able to read it.

And what he read made him turn as white as the hollyhocks outside the front door.

CHAPTER 8

The clock did not have numbers on it like an ordinary clock. There were no 'one to twelve' figures. Where one o'clock should be, this clock said eleven and where twelve o'clock should be, this clock said twenty-two.

All the numbers, Henry realised after a pause for thought, had had ten added to them; one became eleven, two became twelve, three became thirteen and so on.

There might well have been a very simple explanation for this, but for one other mystery. Beside each number was a small 'c'.

Perhaps, thought Henry, 'c' stood for some electrical word. He began thinking of all the strange 'c' words he knew – centigrade, centimetre, centipede. And then he saw it, printed across the c-for-centre of the clock's face, the word

century

in tiny gold letters.

'C for century!' said Henry out loud and at precisely the same moment he heard the sound of the front door key and the voices of Aunt Agatha and Mr Perkins.

Henry jumped up from the bed, pulled the cover straight and ran down the stairs. Aunt Agatha and Mr Perkins had both been 'stocking up'. But it wasn't the usual just-about-enough sort of stocking up. There were boxes and boxes of food. Such food as had never been seen before at 131 Ballantyre Road – lemonade, shortbread biscuits, crisps, a block of ice cream, a bag of cherries, and a dozen fat, juicy oranges.

In normal circumstances, Henry would have been overjoyed by this great shopping bonanza. But now, although he felt quite mouth-wateringly hungry as he helped to unpack the boxes, and although he suddenly thought that Mr Perkins was quite the nicest person he had ever known, Henry, for once, could not keep his mind on food.

Centuries, he was thinking, a clock that tells the time not in hours, minutes and seconds, but in centuries. What happened with such a clock if you re-set it – say, for the eleventh century, or the twenty-second century? And, more importantly, what did Harvey Angell want with such a clock? How did he use it and what did he use it *for*?

It occurred to Henry that perhaps both he and Aunt Agatha – indeed, perhaps everyone in the house – had something wrong with their hearing and that Harvey Angell had not said he was an Electr-ician. No, he had said he was a Mag-ician.

'What time will Mr Angell be home?' he asked Aunt Agatha impatiently.

'In time for supper, I suppose,' said Aunt Agatha.

'What time did he go to work this morning?' Henry asked next.

'You're very interested in the comings and

goings of this fellow,' said Mr Perkins. 'If you ask me . . .'

'We weren't asking you, Mr Perkins,' said Aunt Agatha crisply. 'It was about six o'clock. I know because he brought me a cup of tea before he went out.'

'Brought you a cup of tea!' spluttered Mr Perkins. 'You mean he had the cheek to come into your bedroom and bring you a cup of tea?'

'It was very thoughtful,' said Aunt Agatha. 'Others would do well to follow Mr Angell's example when it comes to diet, working hours and thoughtfulness.'

'I suppose it isn't thoughtful doing all this shopping for you,' said Mr Perkins, 'and it isn't thoughtful digging and scything and mowing and weeding the garden for you.'

'Well, when it comes to the shopping,' said Aunt Agatha, 'I would say that it is half thoughtful and half self-interest. And as for the garden . . . gardening is good for the poetic muse. Far better than idling your time away in the library.'

Mr Perkins huffed and puffed at this, but Aunt Agatha sent him off with a load of potatoes to put in the vegetable basket. Henry put the biscuits in the tin, only half listening to Aunt Agatha and Mr Perkins.

He was wondering what to do next. He could, of course, march right up to Mr Angell and say, 'I know. I know about the clock. I know you are not really an electrician.' But to do that meant confessing that he'd been spying in Harvey Angell's attic. Henry felt bad about that now. He realised that he'd only been pretending to want to look after Aunt Agatha and it was a bad kind of pretence. He had really been overwhelmingly curious.

Also, to confess now meant risking goodness knows what. Or perhaps goodness knows watt. Watts and volts, watts and volts; better by far than thunderbolts.

An alternative was to tell Aunt Agatha everything. But would she believe him? Henry thought not. Aunt Agatha was much improved, but it didn't take much to make the old wintery withers turn her to ice again. Besides, the only person capable of melting Aunt Agatha's ice seemed to be Harvey Angell himself.

Anyway, Henry didn't really want to tell on Harvey Angell. He couldn't forget Harvey Angell's smile or the good cheer that seemed to have followed Harvey Angell like a happy dancing shadow – if shadows could be said to be happy.

If there's an opportunity at supper, thought Henry, I shall turn the conversation to the subject of clocks.

But there wasn't an opportunity. Everyone else – except Harvey Angell and Henry – was very chatty at supper time. Mr Perkins talked at length about all the plants he'd found in the garden. Miss Muggins said she'd been to the Oxfam shop and bought *The News Chronicle Song Book* and she hoped Aunt Agatha would play the songs for her. Miss Skivvy said she'd been to the library and borrowed a book of poems and she was going to learn another one off by heart as they'd enjoyed *The Forsaken Merman* so much.

Harvey Angell smiled once or twice and whenever he did, Henry thought, he can't be bad.

He just can't be! After supper Harvey Angell said he had a lot of research to do and went straight to the attic.

'Perhaps I can help,' Henry heard himself saying in a rather high and squeaky voice.

'Not now, Henry,' said Aunt Agatha. 'I'm going to give you your first piano lesson.'

'Another time,' said Harvey Angell and he smiled at Henry. It was the big 500 kilowatt smile.

Henry smiled back, he just couldn't help himself.

The piano lesson seemed to take at least three centuries.

'I don't think I've got piano fingers,' Henry protested after the first ten minutes.

'Nonsense!' said Aunt Agatha. 'You just haven't learnt how to use them properly. No, don't stick them out straight like that, bend them, bend at the knuckles. And don't droop your wrists! Up with them! Up!'

Aunt Agatha tried to teach Henry a tune called *Up and Down the Stairs* which he played first with his right hand and then with his left. Henry was itching to try the very bottom notes of the piano and the very top ones.

'This is a rather small staircase,' he said. 'Can't I go right down to the dungeon and then up to the tower?'

'All right,' said Aunt Agatha.

So with rather stiff fingers, Henry climbed down to the dungeon at the bottom of the keyboard. The notes were wonderfully boomy and gloomy. Then he climbed to the top of the piano where the sounds were light, almost magical chimes, as if you'd climbed up above the clouds, Henry thought, or up to Harvey Angell's attic and the mysterious Centuries Clock.

'What was the song Miss Muggins sang?' asked Henry. 'The sad one about the old people? Can I play that?'

'*The Old Folks at Home*,' said Aunt Agatha and she hummed it to him. Henry picked out the tune with one finger. He felt immensely pleased with himself. As pleased as if he'd just discovered some kind of treasure that had always been there, waiting for him.

Aunt Agatha nodded approvingly. 'You've got your great-grandma's ear,' she said.

'Have I?' said Henry, trying to feel the shape of his left ear.

Aunt Agatha laughed. 'No, I meant you have a good musical ear. Grandma Ellie had perfect pitch. You only had to name a note and she could sing it.'

Talking of Great-Grandma Ellie made Henry look up at the two photographs on top of the piano – Aunt Agatha as a bride and Aunt Agatha holding a baby in her arms.

Henry, his arms aching with the effort of holding his wrists up as Aunt Agatha commanded, said, 'Who is the baby, Aunt Agatha?' He was quite unprepared for his aunt's response.

Aunt Agatha slammed down the lid of the piano so fast that Henry only just pulled his fingers out in time.

'That's not something I want to talk about. Not now. Not ever!' said Aunt Agatha. And it was the old Aunt Agatha. Aunt Agatha as she had been before the coming of Harvey Angell, before she'd thrown away the key of the piano, Aunt Agatha of the wintery withers.

'I'm terribly sorry, Aunt Agatha, I didn't ...'
Mean to upset you, he was going to say. But Aunt
Agatha had risen from her chair by the piano and
was collecting up the supper dishes, making the
noise of a small army.

'Enough!' she said. 'Enough! It's time you were
in bed, Henry.'

Henry hesitated. 'Will we play again, Aunt
Agatha?' he asked. 'I know I wasn't very good,
but I enjoyed it. I'm sure I'd like it more when I
can play a tune.'

'Henry, just lately you've been asking far too
many questions,' snapped Aunt Agatha. 'Now GO
TO BED!'

Henry went, but it was difficult to sleep.
There were too many things he couldn't
understand. Too many problems he didn't know
how to solve.

Henry thought about Aunt Agatha's sudden
anger over the photograph. Why had it upset
her so much, his asking about the baby? He
remembered she had said there were 'three things
your great-grandma Ellie never got over.' And

then she had told him two of them. A daughter upping and offing, a granddaughter – Henry's own mother – dying, but there had been another sorrow in between those two. What was it? Was it to do with the baby in the photograph? And how was he to find out if Aunt Agatha refused to talk about it?

Henry sighed and turned over in bed. But it was as if there was one problem – the Aunt Agatha problem – on one side of him, and the other problem – the Harvey Angell problem – on the other side, and no sleep for Henry stuck, like the unknown sorrow, in the middle of them.

He sat up in bed and reached for the notebook he used at school for rough work. There were plenty of blank pages at the back of it.

'CLUES TO THE MISTERY OF HARVEY ANGELL,' wrote Henry at the top of the page. (Did the word 'mistery' come from a mixture of mist and misery? wondered Henry. If so it was a very good word to describe how he felt right now. Miserable and unable to see clearly.)

'Clock,' he wrote down next. And then, 'Conneckshuns and Conneckting Kit.'

Here he paused for a long time. 'Connections' was a word that Harvey Angell used a lot. What had he said on his first day in the house when Aunt Agatha was questioning him? 'I don't like to live in a house where there isn't a child. No connections, you see.'

So he, Henry, was some sort of connection. The sort of connections Harvey Angell was interested in did not seem to be electrical ones. They were not to do with wires and sockets. There had been, thought Henry, quite a lot of connecting – of a different sort – going on in the house. All the other lodgers, for instance, were much more friendly to each other than before. And he, Henry, had made a connection with his own past, with his mother and his great-grandmother. He had tried – and failed – to make a connection between the old Aunt Agatha he knew and the young Aunt Agatha of the photographs. But what had all this to do with Harvey Angell and his Connecting Kit?

Henry gave up on it. He tried another word. 'Sirkit,' wrote Henry.

Harvey Angell had made Mr Perkins very angry

with that word. 'Poets are very like electricians,' he'd said. 'We're on the same circuit.'

It was all too much for Henry's head. His thoughts seemed to be going round and round the same circuit and getting nowhere. He put down the pad and pencil and reached for his alarm clock.

Tomorrow morning was Saturday. He would follow Harvey Angell's example all right, just as Aunt Agatha said he should. He would get up early and follow him to the Energy Fields. Whatever Harvey Angell was up to in the house had to be *connected* to what he was doing outside the house.

He set the alarm clock for 5.45 a.m. He hoped the Energy Fields weren't far away. He would need to be back in time for breakfast or Aunt Agatha would suspect that something was wrong. At least breakfast was an hour later on Saturdays, nine instead of eight o'clock.

He was just dropping off to sleep when he heard angry voices above him. Aunt Agatha and Mr Perkins. Henry propped himself up on one elbow and listened.

'But you *must* have found it,' Aunt Agatha was yelling. 'When you were out there this morning, scything and mowing.'

'Well, what if I did,' Mr Perkins yelled back. (Mr Perkins, mild Mr Perkins, yelling!) 'Finders keepers!'

'It is my key and I want it back!' cried Aunt Agatha.

'You are a bully,' shouted Mr Perkins, 'and if you think I'm going to give you the key back so that you can lock everything up again – lock up the piano, lock up laughter, lock up your heart – then you are very much mistaken!'

Henry wanted to cheer. Good old Mr Perkins!

A door slammed upstairs and then there was silence. Henry looked at his alarm clock. He felt very glad it had ordinary numbers on it and ordinary fingers pointing to eleven o'clock. Seven hours to go, then – the Energy Fields.

CHAPTER 9

Henry zapped his alarm clock very quickly before it could wake Aunt Agatha. He lay still, listening. A sleepy silence held the house, only interrupted by the occasional snorting snore from Aunt Agatha's room. Then there was movement! Creaks on the stairs! The sound of someone whistling in the kitchen. Harvey Angell was up and about, preparing for the Energy Fields.

Henry slid out of bed, pulled on his jeans and shirt and waited. He would wait until he heard the front door close, then he would count twenty, then he would be off, following Harvey Angell. Henry's mouth felt very dry. He wished he could go into the kitchen for a drink of water. He put on his trainers. Someone must have been thinking of spies and detectives when they invented trainers. They were wonderfully quiet. There it was! The catch on the front door turning, then the click as Harvey Angell closed it quietly behind him.

Henry meant to count to twenty slowly but it came out in a kind of breathless gabble and then he was out in the dawn grey street and Harvey Angell had just reached the first corner of Ballantyre Road.

There was no one else about. Curtains were still drawn on the sleeping houses. A few cats were savaging black plastic rubbish bags for scraps. In the distance Henry could hear the whine of a milk float. He was glad of that. He felt suddenly and horribly alone. What if Harvey Angell should turn round, see him and hurl a quick thunderbolt?

Harvey Angell did not look – from the back of him anyway – as if he were thinking of throwing thunderbolts at anyone. He walked with an easy bounce. He carried a bag over one shoulder, a bag embroidered with stars, and the bag bounced as Harvey Angell walked. Walked and whistled.

They had turned right and then left and then left again when Henry became aware of someone walking behind him. It made his back feel stiff and bony. And what an awful thing to happen! Here he was following Harvey Angell and now there was someone following him! The follower being followed.

Henry tried the tricks he'd seen on television. Walking slowly to see if the footsteps slowed too. (They did!) Stopping altogether to see if the following footsteps stopped. (They did!) Hurrying. So did the follower. Henry sneaked a quick look over his shoulder as he – with Harvey Angell ahead of him – turned another corner. Henry saw a man in a long grey mac, a hat pulled down low over his eyes and a scarf masking his face.

Horrors! Here he was trapped between them, between Harvey Angell ahead and this other, distinctly suspicious-looking character, behind. In a panic Henry considered his options. Should he run and catch up with Harvey Angell? Confess all? Say that he wanted to see the Energy Fields? Risk it, risk Harvey Angell being a force for good rather than evil? What was it Aunt Agatha sometimes said – 'Better the devil you know than the one you don't.' But just thinking of devils made Henry even more scared.

The awful thought occurred to Henry that the man following him might be in league with Harvey Angell. That the two of them might be part of a large criminal gang, perhaps out to capture the Power Station of the country and hold the Prime Minister to ransom. It was possible, too, that in some mysterious way Harvey Angell had known that Henry planned to follow him and had arranged to have him, Henry followed – and, thought Henry with a sinking heart, probably disposed of, kidnapped and kept in a dungeon. In his heart Henry heard the echo of the piano's doomy, gloomy bottom-of-the-keyboard notes.

He was on the point of giving up. At the next corner I'll make a dash for it, he thought. I'll go home and work out some other plan. He took one more look behind him. The stranger was still there – but was lifting his hat and waving it, waving it frantically at Henry. Henry stared and stared again. It couldn't be! It wasn't! It was! Mr Perkins!

Henry stopped and Mr Perkins, his mac flapping about him, came huffing and puffing up to join him. Of one accord they kept going together, hurrying after Harvey Angell, talking in urgent whispers as they went.

'Whatever are you doing?' hissed Henry.

'I might ask you just the same,' panted Mr Perkins.

'Why are you all dressed up like that?'

'I'm being a detective,' said Mr Perkins. 'This is how detectives dress, isn't it?'

'It is if you want everyone to know you're being a detective,' said Henry.

'I'm following him,' said Mr Perkins, pointing ahead at Harvey Angell who swung along in front of them in happy innocence, the starry bag bouncing on his back.

'So am I,' said Henry.

'A highly suspicious character,' said Mr Perkins. 'Or should I say a sniff-picious character. Always sniffing about the place. Making strange remarks. I thought it was my duty to protect your Aunt

Agatha. Within the tough exterior of your Aunt Agatha is a very tender soul. Oh yes, a very tender soul.'

Henry had no wish to discuss Aunt Agatha's tender soul at that moment, even if she had one. Which he doubted.

'Where d'you think he's going?' he asked.

They had reached the centre of town now. There were one or two people about, mainly newspaper boys and nurses on early shift at the hospital.

'Goodness knows,' said Mr Perkins. 'But I don't believe one word of all that electrical nonsense. And I'll tell you one thing, we are not heading for the offices of the Electricity Board. They are in the High Street, next to the bank.'

'He says he does research in the Energy Fields – whatever they are,' said Henry.

'Energy Fields, my eye!' said Mr Perkins. 'And my nose and ear. He's part of a criminal gang is my thinking.' And Mr Perkins put his hat back on and pulled it down over his eyes.

'You make an awful detective,' said Henry

crossly. 'You did much better pretending to work at the bank.'

'Did I?' asked Mr Perkins, looking quite pleased. 'Did I do that well?'

'Very well,' said Henry. 'But come on – quick! He's going down there!'

They had reached the far end of the town now, near the river and just by the old Cathedral. Henry had been there once to do brass rubbings. Behind them they could hear the great bell in the University tower boom the hour. It was a ten ton bell, Henry had been told at school, and it was called Great George. In the still streets, the six o'clock struck by Great George had a doom-laden sound, as if it sounded the Day of Judgement.

Harvey Angell quickened his pace. Henry almost had to trot to keep up with him and Mr Perkins was puffing and panting in a most undetectively way.

'I think he's going there,' said Henry. 'I think he's going to the Cathedral! Perhaps that's what he does every morning. Goes to church. We never thought of that.' He felt suddenly very disappointed. It was true that he did not want Harvey Angell to be a Force for Evil. But nor did he want him to be a boring old goody-goody!

'No, he's not,' said Mr Perkins. 'He's going around the back. Duck! He's looking round!' They both ducked down under the Cathedral wall.

When they peered out again Mr Perkins said, 'Well, I never! Well, I never!'

'He's going into the graveyard!' said Henry, and the biggest shiver he had ever shivered went right down him from the back of his neck to the end of his toes.

'Round the side!' urged Mr Perkins, becoming very efficient. 'There's a bigger wall round there. And a yew tree. We can hide quite easily. And watch. I think we've stumbled on some Black Magic here!'

Bending low, they ran round the side of the Cathedral until they were by the graveyard. They found a place in the old wall where the uneven stones allowed them to climb up high enough to see into the graveyard and yet jump down quickly.

Henry was first up.

HarveyAngell sat on a tombstone – a tombstone with a marble angel at one end of it – eating a sandwich and looking about him as if enjoying the view of gloomy graves, the dark trees lining the path, the clearing dawn sky.

'It's a funny thing,' said Mr Perkins in a slow whisper, 'but he somehow looks very at home here.' Henry had to agree.

When Harvey had finished his sandwich he stood up and stretched. And then, to the astonishment of his watchers, he began doing his exercises.

'My!' said Mr Perkins enviously. 'He's really supple, he is. Look at him now! He's standing on his head!'

And indeed this was so. Harvey Angell could balance perfectly on his head for minutes on end, so it seemed. And when he'd finished standing on his head he stood up very straight and tall, raised his arms to the sky and then bowed, very low. Three times he raised his arms, stretched and bowed.

'This could be some kind of pagan sun-worshipping rite!' said Mr Perkins.

'Getting the energy from the sun,' said Henry.

'It can't be sunny every day,' said Mr Perkins. 'Yesterday it was pouring with rain.'

When he'd finished his exercises, Harvey Angell walked up the tree-lined path.

'Well, now I know he's bats,' said Mr Perkins. 'Utterly and completely bats! He's hugging all the trees!'

And it was true. Harvey Angell walked lightly but solemnly up and down the path, hugging each and every tree as he went.

'Tree energy?' said Henry hopefully. 'He's getting energy out of the trees.'

'You're as daft as he is,' said Mr Perkins. 'All he'll get is a very grubby T-shirt.'

When he'd finished hugging the trees Harvey Angell began walking about the graves. He produced a small trowel from his knapsack and began weeding round some of the stone slabs. There was a tap in one corner of the graveyard. Harvey Angell filled a watering can that stood nearby and began watering the pots of flowers people had left on the graves.

'I don't think I like this,' said Mr Perkins.

'This is all too spooky for me. Any minute now he's going to begin talking to those – those dead bodies in there. I can feel it in my bones.' Mr Perkins looked quite tearful.

But Henry felt curiously calm. The Cathedral stood over them. In some way he could never have explained, its oldness seemed protective. And although Harvey Angell's behaviour was odd, decidedly odd, it was somehow nice. Kindly and nice. It occurred to Henry that perhaps his mother might be buried under one of those gravestones (he hoped someone had given her a great, grand marble angel, but Aunt Agatha was probably too mean) and that she would be very pleased if someone like Harvey Angell came in the morning and ate a sandwich or two and hugged the trees and watered the flowers and did a little weeding.

'I don't want to watch any more,' said Mr Perkins, sitting on the ground with his back against the wall. 'You'll have to tell me what he does next.'

But Henry didn't need to tell him what happened next because they could both hear it.

Harvey Angell was playing his flute. The sound, in the spooky graveyard, was unearthly. The flute sang like a superhuman voice. It began as a slow, melancholy song.

'Oh Longfellow and Browning!' exclaimed Mr Perkins. 'Oh Wordsworth, Keats and Blake! That song is enough to waken the dead!'

The shiver went through Henry again. Perhaps, he thought, that is just what Harvey Angell is trying to do. Perhaps that's what he is all about!

And then the song of the flute got merrier and merrier. It became a lilting, dancing sort of song. Henry felt his toes twitching almost uncontrollably. And then something very strange happened to Mr Perkins.

Mr Perkins stood up, tossed his hat into the air, flung off his mac and scarf and bounded over the wall. And there he was in the graveyard in his pyjamas – as Henry now saw – dancing away to Harvey Angell's flute. And Harvey Angell didn't seem at all surprised.

Henry, looking over the wall in astonishment, saw the two of them dancing together. Harvey Angell playing and dancing and Mr Perkins frolicking about as if he'd just joined a junior ballet class. In and out and round and round the graves they danced. And up and down the path and in and out of the trees they twirled and swirled.

Henry was dumbfounded. What had come over Mr Perkins? Mr Perkins who, once upon a time that now seemed several centuries ago, had gone off to his pretend bank all dressed up with his bowler hat and rolled umbrella like the height of respectability? Mr Perkins who had looked then as if he would never, *had* never, *could* never dance!

Electr-ician. Mag-ician! thought Henry again. Harvey Angell had put Mr Perkins, the once quiet and obedient Mr Perkins, under a spell. What was he, Henry, to do? He couldn't leave Mr Perkins to the mercy of Harvey Angell's watts and volts, watts and volts, better by far than thunderbolts, could he? And anyway, the music was getting faster and faster now. It seemed intent on going faster than time itself. And Henry's feet were itching, itching, tingling, hopping, burning to join in.

'Oh, blow it!' said Henry out loud and he climbed

over the wall and joined the dancers. But hardly had he been dancing for a few minutes, he and Mr Perkins, arms linked, whirling about faster and faster, while Harvey Angell laughed at them and played on, than a terrible sadness came over Henry.

At least, he thought afterwards, it hadn't come *over* him, it had come up from inside him, as if it had been there all the time, some dark, uncried-about sorrow. And with the sadness came a dizziness and the flute seemed to be singing like the children of the Forsaken Merman –

Call her once and come away!
This way, this way!

Henry and Mr Perkins both fell to the ground – Mr Perkins shiny-faced and out of breath, Henry with his head whirling and the graveyard spinning about him. The song of the flute seemed to grow first louder then fainter. Mr Perkins hoisted Henry onto his feet and, steadying themselves against each other like a pair of drunks, they looked about them.

Harvey Angell had gone. The music of the

flute drifted back to them. Henry could have wept. He had felt, in the middle of the dance, so close to something. He could not have said what, but something warm, and certain, and right.

Now he felt shivery and sad. He sat down on a gravestone, the one with the large marble angel at the foot of it. It was not the kind of angel Henry wanted.

But Mr Perkins was still elated. 'It must be twenty years since last I danced,' he said, doing a few pirouettes. 'I feel wonderful – just wonderful!'

'But he's gone!' exclaimed Henry angrily. 'And we still don't know what he's up to. We're no wiser.'

'Speak for yourself,' said Mr Perkins, hopping from grave to grave in a way that Henry thought was very childish. 'I feel positively inspired. I can feel a poem coming on. You could say I'd been sparked!' Mr Perkins' laugh rang through the graveyard. 'Sparked!' he repeated, wiping his eyes with the edge of his pyjama jacket. 'The Divine Spark of Inspiration – electricians are called Sparks, you know.'

Henry didn't know. Nor, at that moment, did he care. He was thinking about Harvey Angell's smile, the 500 kilowatt beam. Whoever it was turned upon felt warmed and loved. But afterwards, when Harvey Angell had vanished, like this morning, taking his beam with him . . . what then?

Now that he'd begun dancing, Mr Perkins seemed to have trouble stopping. 'I'll go to the park,' he said in between twirls. 'That's the place for poems. I'm going to write the greatest love poem ever written!'

Gloomily Henry stood up and paced about among the gravestones. He looked down at one of the inscriptions.

'Thomas Quinn,' he read. 'Suddenly Translated from Earth to Heaven on the night of 27th March, 1826.'

Mr Perkins, the divinely sparked Mr Perkins, seemed Suddenly Translated, too. Henry wasn't too sure that he didn't prefer the old, rather cross and complaining Mr Perkins to this new, happily hopping old man with his wisps of hair sticking up on end.

'You can't go to the park in your pyjamas,' said Henry.

'Why not?' asked Mr Perkins. 'All my life I've been pretending to be someone I'm not. I'm very me in pyjamas. Very me indeed.'

Henry, looking at him more carefully, had to admit that this was so. Mr Perkins looked very at home in his yellow and red striped pyjamas.

'Are you coming?' asked Mr Perkins.

'No,' said Henry. 'I'm going to wait here a bit. See if Harvey Angell comes back.' (He didn't for one moment believe that this was likely, but the over-cheerful company of Mr Perkins was more than he could bear.)

Mr Perkins looked momentarily doubtful, as if the poem was pulling him one way and Henry the other. The poem won. 'Well, don't be long,' he said. 'And be sure to get back in time for breakfast.'

Henry nodded. Mr Perkins went hurrying down the road. Henry saw the bright rim of his pyjama trousers flashing red and yellow as Mr Perkins half-walked, half-danced down the street, muttering, 'Moon, tune, June, rune, loon, croon.'

It was suddenly very silent in the graveyard. The sun had risen now and the ivy on the walls glistened with dew. Henry heard a rustling and saw a grey squirrel dash to the top of the wall, its tail like a fat fluffy ruler made for measuring walls and tree trunks. The squirrel paused to look at him and leapt into hiding in a dark yew tree. The squirrel cheered Henry. And now that he had begun looking, he saw that the graveyard was alive with birds – black crows, black and white magpies, two robins and, overhead, a sudden squall of seagulls.

Henry walked round the graveyard once more, reading some of the inscriptions. People died at all ages, he thought, surprised. Here was the grave of Robert James, only four years old. And here was one for Mrs Anne Welch of Aylesbury, 'Who Winged her Flight from this World in Expectation of a Better'.

Henry wondered if his mother had found a better world. If so, it was mean of her to leave him in this one.

With a sigh he left the graveyard and began the walk home. All the excitement of the early morning had left him. He felt tired, hungry and disappointed. And the route home seemed to take forever.

He was nearly there – two more left turns and he'd be in Ballantyre Road – when he saw a café he had never noticed before. At least he didn't so much see it, at first, as smell it.

Someone had just gone in and, as the door opened and closed, a wonderful bacon, egg and toast breakfast smell curled out as if the morning itself had just been crisply grilled.

It was the smell that made Henry stop and look. It was odd that he'd never noticed the café before. In the front window there were a great many green ferns and a small statue of a child. The border round the front window of the café was painted dark blue and decorated with gold stars and crescent moons.

Henry looked up at the name of the café. WAIFS AND STRAYS CAFÉ, he read and there, sitting at a table in the window, talking and eating at the same time, was Harvey Angell.

CHAPTER 10

The man Harvey Angell was talking to looked like a country man. He had a strong, weather-beaten face as if he'd worked in the fields all his life. The set of his shoulders, the way he held his head tilted to one side as if listening very carefully, gave him a look of great wisdom. Harvey Angell himself appeared much more anxious than usual. He was waving his fork in the air as he spoke and was far too deeply in conversation (and, Henry saw, in bacon and egg) to notice Henry outside.

Henry felt in his pocket and found thirty pence. He could see that wooden partitions, topped by potted plants, divided the café up into booths. It would be easy to slip in without Harvey Angell seeing him. Another customer left, followed by a second whiff of bacon. Henry hesitated no longer.

The door jangled as he went in but he was small enough not to be seen over the partition and luck was on his side: the booth next to Harvey Angell's was empty. Glad of the potted ferns and spider plants that provided extra cover, Henry slid into a seat.

The café was curiously dark. There were more stars and crescent moons on the ceiling. Henry noticed too that there were a lot of paintings on the walls – all of them houses – large, grand houses, thin terraced houses, cottages, bungalows, blocks of flats.

A waitress came to take his order. Henry, who had never ordered for himself in a café before, suddenly felt nervous. 'I've got thirty pence,' he blurted out.

'That's all right, love,' said the girl, wiping the table with a damp cloth. 'You can have a nice cup of hot chocolate for that.' She took out a small pad and wrote it down. 'Waif, Stray or Homer?' she asked.

Henry felt bewildered. What did she mean? 'I don't think I'm any of those,' he said. (What on earth *was* a Homer?)

The girl tucked the pencil behind her ear. 'You must be *one* of 'em' she said, 'otherwise you wouldn't have got in.'

Henry was at the point of saying that he had got in quite easily by just opening the door, and then decided against it. If this was a café Harvey Angell came to regularly, you could be watts-and-volts sure that there was something extraordinary about it.

'I'm a Stray,' said Henry, attempting a smile.

'Right you are, love,' said the waitress. 'Back in a jiffy. Or should I say "back in a hot chocolate"?'

Henry was glad that was over. He'd been worried that Harvey Angell might hear and recognise his voice.

He sat back and strained his ears to listen to the conversation going on in the next door booth.

'There's progress,' he heard Harvey Angell say, 'but something's blocking the final connection.'

'You can't always succeed in making that final connection,' said the old man. 'And if you don't, it will go down in the records as 'Second Visit Required'.

'But that won't be for ages,' protested Harvey Angell.

'Let me see,' said the old man. There was the sound of a book being consulted, pages turned. 'It would be in the year 2090,' he said.

'Exactly!' said Harvey Angell. (He sounded quite angry, Henry thought.) 'Far too late for the boy.'

'But not, perhaps, for the boy's boy,' said the old man gently.

What on earth were they talking about, wondered Henry? Was he the boy? And who was the boy's boy? He missed the next bit of conversation because the waitress arrived back with his hot chocolate. It came with a thick slice of buttery toast.

'Special for Strays,' she said, giving him a wink. Henry felt terribly guilty but the toast, with the butter soaking through it to the underside, looked delicious – and perhaps, after all, he was a kind of Stray. He gave the girl his thirty pence.

'It's all very well thinking in centuries,'

Harvey Angell was saying crossly, 'but my motto is, "Look after the moment and the centuries will look after themselves".'

'True, true,' said the old man – Henry could almost see him nodding. 'But you know the rules. No trespassing against time. Sorrow must work its own way out.'

'It's the source of sorrow that's the problem,' said Harvey Angell.

'Sorrow often hardens,' said the old man sadly.

'I just need more time,' pleaded Harvey Angell.

'Experience has shown that to continue beyond the allotted time is only to make matters worse,' said the old man. 'But it sounds hopeful to me. You've made some connections and the piano's open, you say?'

'Oh yes . . . I've got *that* going, all right!'

The old man laughed. His laugh, thought Henry, was like Harvey Angell's smile. Warming. 'I'll see what I can do,' said the old man.

'Fine!' said Harvey Angell. He must certainly be smiling the 500 kilowatt smile. 'Let's have some more coffee and toast.'

It was the moment to go, thought Henry. He drained the last of the chocolate and slipped out behind the partition and out of the door. The waitress waved at him. Henry gave her a brief wave back and darted down the street.

His head felt as if it was bursting with all the strange things he had heard. And bursting with questions, too. One thing was now perfectly clear. He had not been imagining things. Harvey Angell was no ordinary lodger. He had come to 131 Ballantyre Road for some particular reason – on a very particular mission. And it was to do with making connections. Then there was the mysterious stuff about time and not trespassing. And sorrow. Rather a lot about sorrow, Henry thought as he hurried home. For some reason the photograph on top of the piano came back into his mind and Aunt Agatha slamming down the piano's lid when he'd asked about the baby and refusing to talk about it – 'Not now. Not ever!' That's what she'd said.

Was the 'source of sorrow' to do with the photograph? Could he tell Harvey Angell about it? It would mean confessing about the café –

and probably about looking at the Connecting Kit. Would Harvey Angell be angry?

And who, Henry wondered, was the old man in the café? Indeed, who were the people who went to the café? What had the waitress meant when she'd asked him if he was a Waif, a Stray or a Homer?

Henry felt twice as confused as he had been when he'd started out, at dawn, to follow Harvey Angell to the Energy Fields.

The sound of Aunt Agatha banging the breakfast gong as he slipped in the door of 131 Ballantyre Road was comfortingly normal.

CHAPTER 11

There was no sign of Harvey Angell at breakfast. Nor of Mr Perkins. Presumably he was still in the park being divinely sparked, thought Henry. Perkins the Park Spark – why, he might be turning into a poet himself!

Miss Skivvy hurried off straight after breakfast saying that she was going to visit her cousin for the day.

'I'm going out too, Henry,' said Aunt Agatha. 'It's my market day, remember?'

Henry hadn't remembered. He'd far too many other things to think about than Aunt Agatha's trip to the market. Once a month, on a Saturday, she went, filling a basket with old clothes – she seemed to have an unlimited supply of these – which she sold and then went on to buy other clothes. It was a good day for her if she made a profit and a bad one if she made a loss.

Henry was usually glad of a Saturday free from Aunt Agatha, but today he felt so bothered and bewildered that he didn't want to be on his own.

'Oh,' he said, 'I'd forgotten it was market day. I was hoping we could have another piano lesson, Aunt Agatha.'

'Certainly not,' said Aunt Agatha, stuffing her basket full of tatty, grey-looking skirts and jerseys with holes in the elbows. 'That whole musical episode was a big mistake. I don't know what came over me.'

'Whatever it was, it was rather nice,' said Henry. 'And you're so good at the piano, Aunt Agatha.'

But Aunt Agatha wasn't to be won over by flattery. (Unless, thought Henry gloomily, it was accompanied by the bewitching smile of Harvey Angell.)

'That's all in the past. And it's no good trying to bring the past back. If that wretched Mr Perkins would give me back the key of the piano, I'd lock it up again. There are a lot of things in life that are – that are too painful – better kept locked up.'

'What sort of things?' asked Henry, quick as a flash. 'Do you mean the other sad thing in the story of Great-Grandma Ellie?'

'Henry, I've told you before about asking too many questions,' said Aunt Agatha. 'Now, I shall miss all the bargains unless I hurry. I'm sure you have plenty of homework to do. I expect to see it finished when I get home. I've left you a cold pork pie in the fridge for lunch.'

And then Aunt Agatha was gone, her bulging basket of clothes over her arm. The hollyhocks shuddered as she banged the front door behind her.

'I'm afraid I'm going out, too,' said Miss Muggins apologetically to the glum Henry. 'But I've got an hour to spare. Shall I go and get my *News Chronicle Song Book*? If I sang some of the songs, you could pick out the tunes on the piano?'

'Oh, yes please,' said Henry, cheering up at once.

The *Song Book* had hundreds of songs in it. There were sea-shanties and folk songs and hymns and carols Henry knew from school.

Miss Muggins set the book on the piano and sang. She would sing half a verse and then Henry would pick out the tune on the piano. When he went wrong, Miss Muggins would repeat it again and again until they could do it together, Miss Muggins singing, Henry playing.

'I do wish I could do two hands,' said Henry.

'I'm sure you could if you had a few lessons,' said Miss Muggins.

They worked their way through *God Save the Queen, Little Brown Jug, Abide with Me* and *Good King Wenceslas.* 'I don't think we have to wait for Christmas to sing a carol,' said Miss Muggins.

Henry's favourite song was *Robin Adair.* Miss Muggins sang all three verses, putting great feeling into the last one.

> But now thou'rt cold to me,
> Robin Adair.
> But now thou'rt cold to me,
> Robin Adair.

Yet him I lov'd so well
Still in my heart shall dwell.
Oh! I can ne'er forget
Robin Adair.

It was a song that made Henry think of his mother.

Then Miss Muggins looked at her watch and gave a little shriek. 'Look at the time, Henry! I must be off. I promised to help Mrs Thomas with her ironing. She's broken her arm. And she was expecting me at eleven.'

Henry was surprised to see that it was almost lunch time. The time had flown and he hadn't once thought about the strange morning in the graveyard and the café.

There was still no sign of Harvey Angell. Henry was half glad and half disappointed. He had no idea what to do next about Harvey Angell.

All the questions he'd arrived home with came rushing back like a flock of birds – like the seagulls squalling over the graveyard and temporarily blown away by the piano playing.

Mr Perkins, thought Henry. I need to talk it

over with him. He had heard Mr Perkins come home in the middle of *Abide with Me* and hurry up to his room.

Henry ran up the stairs. But there was a note stuck on Mr Perkins' door. It said POET AT WORK: DO NOT DISTURB. Henry retreated slowly down the stairs. He went back into the kitchen and looked in the fridge. The solitary pork pie sat on a plate with a frill of damp lettuce beside it. Henry shut the fridge door. He remembered he had a pound saved up from his last birthday. There was a fish and chip shop down the road. And . . . there was the café, of course. He could go back there. It was unlikely Harvey Angell or the old man would be there. But there was the friendly waitress. If he asked her, she might tell him more about Homers, Waifs and Strays. And *that* might tell him something about Harvey Angell.

Henry hurried into his room and found his money. He took the pork pie in a bag – it was as hard as a rock, he would throw it away some-where – and hurried down the road.

He felt sure he remembered the way. The café

had been very near Ballantyre Road. If he turned left and then right and right again, that should be it. It was a pity he hadn't noticed the name of the road, but that couldn't be helped. Anyway, with all those stars and moons on the front of it, he couldn't miss it.

But it wasn't left, right and right again.

And it wasn't left, right and left.

Nor was it right, left and left.

Henry asked three people if they knew where the Waifs and Strays Café was but they all looked rather amused and shook their heads.

He must have gone round in a circle by now. He was miles away from the fish and chip shop and he'd thrown away the pork pie. What a perfectly awful Saturday this was. Henry suddenly felt very sorry for himself indeed. Everyone had gone off. No one cared about him at all. If his mother had been alive he supposed that Saturday would have been quite different. They'd have gone to the swimming pool together perhaps, or to the cinema. Saturdays would be special. Probably she would say to him, 'And what would you like to do this afternoon, Henry?'

'You look as if you could do with some lunch,' said a voice beside him, and there was Harvey Angell, beaming the Full Beam.

Henry was so pleased to see him that he quite forgot how angry he'd felt at Harvey Angell's disappearance. He beamed back.

'There's a café just round the corner,' said Harvey Angell. 'I'll take you there.'

They walked briskly round the corner and there it was! The Waifs and Strays Café! Henry gazed at it. He felt sure he'd walked down this street only five minutes ago and that the café hadn't been there then.

'They do wonderful sausages here,' said Harvey Angell, jingling open the door. And suddenly Henry felt very well looked after indeed.

CHAPTER 12

'**Y**ou back again, Mr Angell?' said the waitress as they took their seats. 'You must be having a busy day. And you've got my young hot-chocolate friend with you, I see.'

Harvey Angell raised questioning eyebrows at Henry. Henry blushed.

'You was here this morning, wasn't you, love?' continued the waitress. 'Sitting in this very booth – right next to the one you was in, Mr Angell, with Mr Gabriel. Don't know how you didn't see each other.'

'Maybe one of us didn't want to be seen,' said Harvey Angell, picking up the menu. Henry was relieved to see that he didn't look angry. No watts or volts were likely to fly.

'What's it to be?' asked the waitress. 'We've got two specials today — Supernova Beefburgers and Nirvana Noodles. Oh, and there's Paradise Pudding if you want afters.'

'I'd like Earthly Bangers and Mash,' said Harvey Angell. Henry chose the beefburgers.

'So,' said Harvey Angell, 'you followed me, did you?'

'No,' said Henry. 'Honestly I didn't. After you went off . . .'

'Very impolitely, if I may say so,' interrupted Harvey Angell, 'and I do apologise for that.'

Henry didn't know what to say to this. No adult he had known had ever apologised to him before.

'That's all right,' he said grandly. 'Well, after you'd gone, Mr Perkins went off to the park because he was divinely sparked . . .'

'Divinely sparked . . . ?' echoed Harvey Angell.

'He had a poem coming on,' said Henry. 'It was all that dancing, I think, and the music.'

'It was the Energy, I expect,' said Harvey Angell thoughtfully, 'flowing through him.'

'Whatever it was,' said Henry, eager to get on with his story, 'he went off to the park and I waited a bit and then I walked home. And I saw this café on the way – and you sitting in the window and . . .'

'And you were very curious,' said Harvey Angell. 'I'm not at all surprised, I think you've had a rather puzzling week.'

'I certainly have!' said Henry. 'I've got so many puzzles in my head I don't know which one to ask you about first.'

'Take pot luck!' said Harvey Angell. The waitress had come back with their food. Henry's beefburgers were the fattest and most delicious he had ever tasted. They came with chips shaped into stars and crescent moons.

'Well, this café,' said Henry, through a mouthful of moons, 'I tried and tried to find it again and it just – well, it just wasn't there. Or here. And when I came in this morning the waitress asked me something very strange.'

Harvey Angell raised his eyebrows again.

'She asked me if I was a Waif, a Stray or a Homer.'

'I see,' said Harvey Angell, not looking at all surprised. 'And what did you say?'

'She said I had to be one of them to have got in,' said Henry. 'So I said I was a Stray.'

'I suppose that was true enough, in a way,' said Harvey Angell, demolishing an Earthly Banger. 'You've sort of strayed from your world into mine.'

'Please, Mr Angell,' said Henry, putting down his knife and fork, 'what *is* your world? And what is this café about? And what is a Homer? And why did you go to the graveyard this morning? And who was the old man and . . .'

'Steady on,' said Harvey Angell, laughing. 'I can see it's time for some explanations. But I can only answer one question at a time.' He finished his sausages and mash, wiped his mouth slowly and carefully and began.

'My world, Henry,' he said, 'is the world of the Homers. That's what I am. A Homer.'

'I thought you were an electrician,' said Henry, his doubts rising again.

'To be a Homer you have to be an electrician, too,' said Harvey Angell.

'And I thought Homer was a famous Greek man,' said Henry, eating the last starry chip.

Harvey Angell laughed again. 'Yes, a famous poet. Poets and electricians again. But I'm not that kind of Homer. My job is to make people feel at home. To make unhomely houses into homes. That's what we Homers do.'

'I don't understand,' said Henry.

'Patience!' said Harvey Angell. 'You see, some houses – houses like yours in Ballantyre Road – well, they aren't proper homes. There's something sad about them. They are just houses, sad houses where people eat and sleep. They aren't homes. They aren't connected.'

Ah! There was that word again! Henry thought back to the Connecting Kit and how he'd tried to puzzle out what Harvey Angell meant by the word 'connecting'.

'You mean,' he said, 'that nobody in the house is friendly. It's a sort of cold and lonely house. Like 131 was before you came?'

'Yes,' said Harvey Angell. 'That's a large part of it – but only part.'

Henry hoped this wasn't going to become

like his conversation with Aunt Agatha, when he'd only learnt part of the story. Grown-ups, he thought, were very good at giving you only part of a story. Like giving you a jigsaw with the most important pieces missing, the pieces that made the picture make sense.

'Well, what's the other part?' he asked now.

'That's where the electrics come in,' said Harvey Angell. 'It's to do with the circuit.'

There was that other word that had puzzled Henry so much. He had looked it up in the dictionary but hadn't been able to find it because he thought it began with 's' and, as he found out by looking in his Junior Science Encyclopaedia, it began with a 'c'. Dictionaries weren't much good unless you could already spell, thought Henry. But once he'd found the spelling, he'd looked up the meaning of the word.

'Circuit', said the dictionary, meant 'a journey round' (Henry felt he had been on one of these lately – round and round in puzzles and unfinished stories). Or, said the dictionary, it could refer to a judge who went round and round the courts of England, or a preacher who went on a circuit of parishes of the country. Lastly, said the dictionary, a circuit was 'the path of an electric current'.

Henry was pleased to show off his new-found dictionary knowledge.

'I know about circuits,' he said. 'They are journeys round and round. Or the path of an electric current.'

'Well done!' said Harvey Angell. 'If you mix those two together you get the kind of circuit I'm interested in.'

Henry frowned. 'Do you go on a roundabout journey seeing to people's electric currents?' he asked.

'Not quite,' said Harvey Angell. 'What I do is connect the living and the dead. We're all on the same circuit, you see. Only people forget that. They switch off, like you switch off an electric light. When you switch off an electric light you break the circuit. You break the connection to the electric current.'

Henry got The Shiver again. He was glad of the Supernova Beefburgers. He didn't know if he could cope with a circuit between the living and the dead on anything less than a full stomach. But Harvey Angell spoke so matter-of-factly about it that it was comforting. It was as if the dead – people like his mother – weren't really dead-dead, not existing, but somehow simply not to be seen. Gone on a roundabout journey, a journey round the circuit.

Even so, there was still a lot he didn't understand.

'Are you saying there's an electric current that comes from dead people?' he asked. (He felt very glad that they were having this conversation in the middle of the day and not at night. He didn't like to think of all those bodies in the graveyard giving out electric shocks.)

But Harvey Angell laughed. 'No,' he said. 'Not the sort of electric current that makes the fridge or the radio or the lights work. What I mean is an energy. Energy in people is – well – it's the same as love. It can't turn on radios and cookers, but it can make people light up. It can make homes and churches. It can make paintings and poems and music.'

'Energy is eternal delight,' said Henry,

suddenly remembering the poem Harvey Angell had quoted.

'You've got it!' said Harvey Angell.

'And it doesn't die when a person dies?'

'Definitely not,' said Harvey Angell. 'It passes on into other people. It passes on into thoughts that go on a circuit from person to person. You can find it in a piece of much-loved furniture. Sometimes it glows, not just with the polish but with the love rubbed in with the polish. The energy someone's put into it.'

'Like Great-Grandma Ellie's dresser,' said Henry.

'Absolutely. Your great-grandma must have loved that dresser a lot.'

'And that explains the reference,' said Henry. 'The one you gave to Aunt Agatha which said, "He works with great energy".'

'Oh, that!' said Harvey Angell modestly. 'I just do what I can. But I always need a child around. Children aren't switched off like adults. Sorrow makes people switch off.'

'Is Aunt Agatha switched off?' asked Henry. 'And Mr Perkins and Miss Muggins and Miss Skivvy?'

'Well, they *were*,' said Harvey Angell. 'But Mr Perkins is definitely connected again now. And Miss Muggins and Miss Skivvy – well, I think there's hope for them too. It's your Aunt Agatha who's the difficult one.'

'She's happier than she was,' said Henry.

'Yes, I know,' said Harvey Angell. 'The music has helped. Music always does help in making the connection because music belongs to our time and all time. But Aunt Agatha keeps switching on and off, that's the problem. And until everyone's connected up properly to the Energy Supply – well, it won't be a proper home. I won't have done my job.'

('Second Visit Required,' Henry remembered the old man saying. And the year 2090. Why, he could be in the graveyard himself by then!)

'There's something Aunt Agatha won't talk about,' said Henry. 'Something that makes her sad and cross all at the same time. And it made Great-Grandma Ellie sad, too.'

'I know something of your great-grandma,' said Harvey Angell.

'You do? How?'

'Ah well . . . the tools of my trade . . .' said Harvey Angell.

'The Connecting Kit!' cried Henry. 'The Clock and the Energy Charger! And — now I see — is that why you call the graveyard the Energy Fields? Tell me! Tell me about the Clock. The Century Clock! Harvey, can you go backwards and forwards in time?'

'No, I can't do that exactly,' said Harvey Angell. 'But I can — well, make a connection. In fact it's a lot easier to make a connection with your great-grandma than it is to make one with your Aunt Agatha. Your great-grandma wants you both to be happy, you know. She's got other things to do on the circuit and she can't get on with them until we've sorted out your Aunt Agatha.'

'What shall we do?' asked Henry eagerly. 'And can I help? Will you show me how to use the Connecting Kit? Will you teach me how to be an electrician — a Homer?'

'It's a very long training,' said Harvey Angell. 'And I'm not sure if you'd really want to be a

Homer.' For the first time since Henry had known him, Harvey Angell looked sad.

'You can't have a home of your own if you're a Homer,' he said. 'That's what this café is about. The Waifs and Strays are in training to be Homers. You'd never have seen this café or found it again if it wasn't for me.'

'But I found it this morning,' protested Henry. 'All by myself.'

'Yes. You probably had excess Energy from the dancing,' said Harvey Angell. 'And it was still with you when you walked home.'

'Do you mean I was divinely sparked, too?'

Harvey Angell laughed. 'Well, maybe just a little,' he said. 'But now I've got a question to ask you, Henry. It sounds to me as if you've already had quite a good look at the Clock and the Energy Charger. Might that be true?'

Henry turned scarlet.

'That's all right,' said Harvey Angell. 'I knew you'd find out sooner or later. Well, tonight then. Tonight I'll show you how the Connecting Kit works. But I think I'm going to need your help with Aunt Agatha, OK?'

'OK,' said Henry.

'Shake on it,' said Harvey Angell, holding out his hand. 'Watts and volts!' he said as they shook hands across the table.

'Better by far than thunderbolts!' said Henry.

CHAPTER 13

'**M**idnight,' Harvey Angell said when he and Henry parted outside the Waifs and Strays Café. 'Come up to the attic at midnight.'

Harvey Angell had work to do elsewhere. Henry set off himself for Ballantyre Road. Tonight – tonight at midnight, he was to discover the secrets of the Connecting Kit. Henry ran, hopped, skipped, jumped and all but danced his way home.

He hardly knew what to do with himself when he got there. Aunt Agatha, Miss Muggins and Miss Skivvy were still out. There was total silence from Mr Perkins' room. Probably in a poetic trance, thought Henry.

He went to his room and made a list of the hours until midnight. It was now three o'clock. There were nine hours to go and the first one seemed to last forever.

Henry got out his notebook and turned to the back of it where he had begun writing about Harvey Angell. CLUES TO THE MISTERY OF HARVEY ANGELL, he read, and then the five words underneath – 'Clock, Conneckshuns, Conneckting Kit, Sirkit.' He corrected the spelling of 'circuit' and began writing. 'I am very close to solving the mistery,' he wrote. 'Tonight, at midnight, all will be revealed. This is what I have learnt so far:

1. Harvey Angell is something called a Homer.
2. A Homer's job is to connect the living and the dead.'

Henry put his pen down. Seeing it written down on the page like that made him feel very queer indeed. It was true that this was what Harvey Angell had said, but he'd said it in the snugness of the Waifs and Strays Café and Henry had been eating Supernova Beefburgers at the time.

But the words, put down on the page, looked horribly alarming. All the excitement ebbed out of Henry as if someone had just pulled the duvet off and left him uncovered.

Henry stared at the bald, black-biroed words. Excitement – excess Energy, perhaps – had carried him away, he decided. He'd been so eager to learn about the Connecting Kit, so intrigued to hear about Great-Grandma Ellie being 'on the circuit' that he simply hadn't paused to think things out properly.

Connecting the living and the dead – what else could Harvey Angell mean but GHOSTS!

Now Henry had always liked the *idea* of ghosts. On Halloween, he and James Hussey from up the top of Ballantyre Road dressed up in old sheets and went tricking and treating. Henry had learnt how to make some splendidly spooky wails and groans. But playing ghosts and meeting real ones (if you could call a ghost real) were two different things.

Possibly, thought Henry, with a sudden gloom, Harvey Angell took ghosts for granted. Probably met them every day. Was off now, having a chat with one. Ghosts, to him, were as common as patients to doctors, children to teachers, taps to plumbers – switches to electricians.

Henry saw himself shut up in the attic at midnight while Harvey Angell used all his strange paraphernalia to conjure up spooks, spectres and bogies. Henry went very pale and ghost-like at the thought of this.

The hours had suddenly speeded up. It was five o'clock already. Midnight now seemed far too near.

'I can't go!' Henry said to himself in panic. 'I'll pretend to be ill. When Aunt Agatha comes home, I'll ask her if I can go straight to bed without any supper. Then they'll all believe I'm ill.'

But even as he thought this, Henry knew it wasn't the answer. Never to find out about the Connecting Kit . . . never to learn more about Great-Grandma Ellie and – Henry realised suddenly that this was the important part – never to find out more about his mother. How could he face himself in the mirror again? He would know he was a coward. And besides, Harvey Angell was relying on him for help with Aunt Agatha. Aunt Agatha would remain switched off. 131 Ballantyre Road, the house that had become so much cheerier in the last few days would remain nearly-but-not-quite home, unconnected to the Energy. This was Henry's first adventure and he had failed in it almost before he'd begun.

Tears stung Henry's eyes. And then he had a brainwave. Mr Perkins! He would ask Mr Perkins to come with him to the attic that night. Just the thought of the plumpness of Mr Perkins made Henry feel better. Ghosts couldn't get to you while Mr Perkins was around. However much Mr Perkins might go off on a poetic flight of fancy, there was something very nicely earthed about him. Next to poems, Mr Perkins liked food. Henry couldn't have said why, but a liking for food seemed a very trustworthy trait in another human being.

And surely Harvey Angell wouldn't mind if Mr Perkins came too? Why, they had danced together that very morning! Mr Perkins wasn't quite like other grown-ups and after all, poets and electricians were very alike, weren't they? Harvey Angell had said so himself.

Henry took the stairs to Mr Perkins' room two at a time. He'd forgotten all about the sign on the door. But there it still hung – POET AT WORK. DO NOT DISTURB.

Oh heavens, oh watts and volts and thunder-bolts! thought Henry. Surely a poem couldn't take this long? Mr Perkins had been shut in there for hours and this was an emergency. Henry couldn't live with the idea of going by himself up to the attic for even five more minutes, let alone five more hours. He gave the door a very gentle, apologetic tap.

'Knock and it shall be opened unto thee!' cried Mr Perkins and flung open the door. 'Henry!' he cried, giving Henry a big hug. 'I thought rescue would never come!'

'Rescue?' said Henry, puzzled. 'It says "Do not disturb" on your door.'

'So it does,' said Mr Perkins, looking at the sign. 'It's the wrong way round.' He turned the sign over. Now it read, HELP! POET STUCK IN MID-

POEM. PLEASE RESCUE WITH CONVERSATION, COFFEE OR COMPANY.

'I thought you might be angry,' said Henry.

'On the contrary,' said Mr Perkins, 'I couldn't be more pleased to see you. It's a terrible thing to be stuck in a poem. I feel like Jacob wrestling with an angel. He had to carry on until the angel said, 'Bless you, Jacob'. And that's just what this ungrateful poem won't do. It won't say, 'Thank you, Alfred, for rescuing me from this ream of blank white paper and putting me on the page.' No, not at all. It just wriggles and twists and wants to go its own way.'

Henry said nothing. He felt he was struggling with an angel of his own. Harvey Angell.

'Do you want to hear what I've written so far?' asked Mr Perkins.

'All right,' said Henry reluctantly. When Mr Perkins was excited like this he was rather like a hot air balloon. There was nothing for it but to wait until he drifted quietly down to earth again.

Mr Perkins tossed about a great many sheets of scribbled-upon paper until he found the one he wanted. Then he stood up, hand on heart and declaimed it:

My heart is like your piano keys,
I hear sonatas when you sneeze.
Boiled potatoes, peas and ham,
Love's the pudding, love's the jam.

'What d'you think?'

'Um,' said Henry. 'It doesn't seem to have a beginning.'

'These are the inspirational lines,' said Mr Perkins. 'They probably come in the middle. I'll get the beginning last.'

'I'm not sure about the boiled potatoes,' said Henry.

'Modern poetry!' said Mr Perkins. 'Modern poems are meant to include ordinary domestic things.'

'Oh,' said Henry. 'Well, I'm not sure they go with sonatas.'

'But that's it exactly!' cried Mr Perkins. 'That's just what I'm trying to get at. The lyrical and the humdrum. The ordinary and the extraordinary.'

'I see,' said Henry, and because he could wait no longer to ask for help – 'It's the extraordinary I came to see you about, Mr Perkins.'

'Ah!' said Mr Perkins, putting down his poem at once. 'Harvey Angell, I suppose.'

'Yes,' said Henry. 'I'm meant to go up to his attic at midnight. He's going to show me the Connecting Kit. He's got all sorts of strange things up there, you know – an Energy Charger and a clock that tells the time in centuries, not hours.'

'The hours of folly are measured by the clock; but of wisdom no clock can measure,' said Mr Perkins. 'Blake.'

Henry wriggled. He was fed up with this fellow Blake who seemed to chip in on every important conversation.

'Well, what an adventure!' said Mr Perkins when Henry stayed silent. 'Most boys would give their eye teeth to be in your shoes.'

'I know,' said Henry miserably. 'The trouble is, Mr Perkins – I'm feeling rather scared. I think Mr Angell might be able to conjure up ghosts.'

'Ah!' said Mr Perkins again. 'That's it, is it?'

'Yes,' said Henry, glad to have told his fear at

last. 'And I wondered – I wondered if you would come with me tonight? I'm sure Mr Angell wouldn't really mind. I think he likes poets.'

Mr Perkins smiled. 'That may be so,' he said, 'but I can't come with you, Henry.'

Try as he might, Henry could not stop two tears sliding slowly down his cheeks. He was glad that Mr Perkins seemed not to notice.

'There are some adventures that you have to go on alone,' said Mr Perkins. 'And this sounds like one of them to me.'

'What if I fall out of time?' asked Henry desperately. 'What if Harvey Angell sets the Clock at ten or twenty-two? What if I never get back to this century again?'

'It's a risk,' said Mr Perkins. 'But if you don't take it, how will you feel?'

'Awful!' said Henry.

'There you are, then,' said Mr Perkins. 'And I don't think you need worry too much about ghosts. I always think ghosts are probably more worried about us, like cats are when they suddenly see a human being when they hadn't expected one.'

Henry laughed.

'And if anything really dreadful should happen, just thump on the floor for me. I'm right underneath that attic, you know. And I sleep very lightly.'

'All right,' said Henry. He was feeling much better.

'One other thing,' said Mr Perkins. 'Get some sleep before you go up to the attic. Have something to eat and wrap up warm.'

'There won't be anything to eat after supper,' said Henry. 'You know what Aunt Agatha's like about eating between meals.'

'Here,' said Mr Perkins, rummaging in his cupboard. 'These are my emergency supplies.' He handed Henry a packet of chocolate biscuits.

'Why do I need to wrap up warm?' asked Henry.

'Against the shivers,' said Mr Perkins. 'I always think that that's why knights wore armour. To stop the shivers.'

CHAPTER 14

At midnight, wrapped up warm with a red jersey on top of his pyjamas and wearing his thickest socks, Henry crept up to the attic, carefully avoiding all the stairs that creaked and the loose floorboards outside Miss Skivvy's room.

He had raised his hand to knock, very quietly, on the attic door, when Harvey Angell called, 'Come in!'

Henry went in. Harvey Angell had the window wide open and was gazing out at the stars and the city lights. The Clock – Henry noticed at once – was plugged in and humming like an electric fire warming up. The needle on the Energy Charger leapt to FULL ON as Henry came in and then dropped back, quivering.

'Well done,' said Harvey Angell, turning from the window. 'You've come – and you bring your own youthful Energy with you. That's sure to be a help.'

In what, Henry wanted to ask. But Harvey Angell held up his hand for silence. The Clock had ceased humming. It had begun its erratic slow-then-fast ticking.

'What is it doing . . . ?' Henry began, but stopped, halfway through the question, because suddenly the room was filled with such a sweet, light smell that it almost made Henry dizzy. The smell was like the gentlest summer morning you could ever remember. It was like country hills and dales. It was like the perfect-meadow-for-a-picnic smell.

'Daisies again!' said Harvey Angell crossly. 'I can't seem to get away from daisies. They've been bothering me all night. I've had jasmine, daisies, roses, daisies, bread, daisies, honeysuckle, daisies. Daisies, daisies and daisies. And what we want is apple-blossom.'

Henry, sitting on the edge of the bed, was mystified. 'I don't understand,' he said. 'What *are* all these smells? And why do we want apple-blossom?'

'Because that's your Great-Grandma Ellie's special smell. Her Essence. The smell that belongs to her,' said Harvey Angell, as if this was a perfectly obvious fact that everyone should know.

'To make a connection with your great-grandma we have to sniff her out first. And I've done that. I *know* she's apple-blossom. If I could clear the air of all these daisies we might be able to release the Energy – free the house of sorrow.'

'Are we – are you – going to conjure up any ghosts?' asked Henry in a very small whisper, because despite being wrapped up in his red-jersey-armour, he was still feeling a little shivery.

'Ghosts?' said Harvey Angell, sitting back on his heels. 'Oh no! I don't go in for all that palaver. We'd be here all night if I had to deal with ghosts. Anyway, it's against the rules. No trespassing in time. Rule number twenty-one. Watts and volts! Now we've got bread again. I do hate this one. It makes me feel so hungry.'

'It must be Mr Murgatroyd, the baker,' said Henry. 'Remember? He used to have this room.'

'Ah! That explains it. Sometimes a very recent smell can confuse the Century Clock and then it can't tell the difference between the living and the dead. Mr Murgatroyd, being alive, hasn't changed Essence yet. He might end up being Essence of Lily or Essence of Poppy.'

'He'll be sorry to give up bread,' said Henry who, despite Mr Perkins' chocolate biscuits (eaten earlier), was feeling hungry again at the smell of, and the memory of, Mr Murgatroyd's Granaries, Harvesters and Bloomers. 'How do you know Great-Grandma Ellie is apple-blossom?' he asked as the bread smell drifted away.

'There's always one presiding spirit in the house,' said Harvey Angell. 'If the presiding spirit is switched off, it's an unhappy house. In Madagascar there are some people who say that a soul only really dies if it is left out of the thoughts of the living. To be left out of people's thoughts is to be switched off. Well then, a Homer's job is to release the Energy of the presiding spirit. We're not allowed to deal with anyone else. There's a lot of rules in our trade you know. Just as many as electricians have. You can't go getting your wires crossed and fusing the whole circuit.'

'I see,' said Henry. He felt much comforted to hear that there were rules. Rules were not something Henry had much cared for before. Most of them seemed to begin with the words 'Do not' and carried on to tell you not to do something you very much wanted to do. But when it came to making connections between the living and the dead – well, one or two rules seemed as welcome as signposts in the desert.

'It takes time finding out the presiding spirit,' said Harvey Angell. 'That's what my research has been. The presiding spirit is the one with the strongest and most frequent Essence. And until tonight, when we've had all these wretched daisies, it's always been apple-blossom.'

'But how did you know apple-blossom meant Great-Grandma Ellie?' Henry persisted.

The night was beginning to feel like a strange mathematical dream. Did five apple-blossom smells equal one great-grandma? Express this as a sum. 5AB = 1GG.

'Ah, that's where the detective work comes in,' said Harvey Angell. 'Finding out who that Essence belongs to. Your Aunt Agatha told me.'

'Aunt Agatha?'

'Of course, she didn't know she was telling me,' said Harvey Angell. 'Being switched off herself. But tell me she did. It was when Mr Perkins was doing the garden for her. She gave him particular orders not to touch the apple-blossom. It was Grandma Ellie's favourite, she said.'

'I think we've got daisies again,' said Henry. He noticed that whenever a new smell came into the room the needle of the Energy Charger leapt.

'So we have,' said Harvey Angell. 'I can't understand what's going wrong tonight.'

Henry hesitated to ask a question that might seem rude, but after several minutes of daisies, he couldn't resist it. 'Have you got the Clock on the right time?' he asked.

'Nineteen?' said Harvey Angell. 'Yes, of course that's right. I'm only allowed to turn to the time of the presiding spirit of the house. Your great-grandma was born in 1898 – I found that out from Aunt Agatha too. That means the end of the nineteenth century.'

'So we can't do any time travelling,' said Henry sadly.

'I'm afraid not,' said Harvey Angell, equally sadly. 'I keep getting stuck in the nineteenth century myself. When I got this assignment, I said it was high time I was given a medieval manor or a tudor mansion or something. But no. Orders are orders. It was 131 Ballantyre Road for me.'

'I'm very glad it was,' said Henry shyly.

Harvey Angell gave him the Full Beam. 'Yes,' he said. 'So am I, really. There're not many children to be found in medieval manors or tudor mansions these days. They've all been turned into offices. Mind you, a good Homer can cause havoc in a place like that.' Harvey Angell looked quite dreamy at the thought of playing havoc.

'Why do you go to the graveyard every

morning?' asked Henry. 'Is Great-Grandma buried there?'

'I don't always go to the graveyard,' said Harvey Angell. 'That was just this morning. I go to one or other of the sacred sites where the Energy is strong. That's to re-charge my own Energy. Too much living with the living can dim a Homer's Energy. Graveyards are rather popular with us, I must admit. In fact it's one of the job specifications – a liking for graveyards.'

'I see,' said Henry, a little sadly, thinking that there were a lot of drawbacks to the profession of Homer.

'We must get on,' said Harvey Angell. 'This Clock may work in centuries, but my time is running short.'

'How do we know when we've made a connection – released the Energy?' asked Henry.

'The Essence – the apple-blossom Essence – will sweep through the house. People will turn in their beds and twitch a little as the Energy touches them like a small electric shock. When they wake up in the morning they'll feel as if they've had a really wonderful dream – only they can't quite remember it.'

'And does it make it a happy house after that?' asked Henry.

'Well, yes,' said Harvey Angell. 'But not a and-then-they-lived-happily-ever-after sort of happiness.'

'What sort then?'

Harvey Angell pondered. 'Well,' he said, 'I think I'd call it a not-so-lonely kind of happiness. A belonging kind of happiness – belonging to the past, present and future. A big belonging.'

'It sounds lovely,' said Henry with a sigh. 'I'd like that kind of belonging. Mostly I feel like a plant holding on with its roots to just a teeny bit of soil. How do we make it happen?'

'Well, it's not entirely up to us,' said Harvey Angell.

'What d'you mean?' asked Henry, instantly thinking of ghosts again.

'A Homer is a kind of middle-man between the past and the present,' said Harvey Angell. 'I can't make the connection if there's any resistance – any switching off – on the circuit . . .'

'And there's Aunt Agatha,' said Henry. 'Aunt Agatha with her withering withers.'

Harvey Angell laughed. 'I'm afraid so. I felt we were so nearly there. She has seemed a lot happier – ever since the sing-song really. And I'd hoped with you being here tonight, the combined Energy of Great-Grandma Ellie and you would do the trick.'

'After the sing-song Aunt Agatha went back to her old self again,' said Henry. 'She warmed up and then she withered. She wanted to lock the piano up again, only Mr Perkins wouldn't let her. And when I asked her about the photographs on top of the piano she got all angry and upset again.'

'That's it!' cried Harvey Angell, grabbing Henry's arm. 'The piano! We're in the wrong room! It's all quite obvious. There must be something wrong with my arithmetic that I can't add up properly. Of course! When we had the sing-song last time, Great-Grandma Ellie wasn't part of it. It was just a beginning and it needed you, Henry – the past and the future – to meet! Come on! We're going to have a concert!'

'It's the middle of the night!' exclaimed Henry. 'Aunt Agatha will hit the roof if we start playing the piano now.'

'That might be just what we want!' said Harvey Angell. 'Here! You take the Energy Charger and I'll take the Clock and my flute.' He paused to give Henry the irresistible Full Beam. 'Come on, Henry, this could be the breakthrough!'

CHAPTER 15

It was spooky in the kitchen so late at night. Henry could hear the hollyhocks shushing and hushing outside the window as if they knew something was up. It was a full moon too and the kitchen was held in a scoop of moonlight.

Henry had the feeling that everything in the kitchen – the chairs round the table, the cups hanging on the dresser, the pans on the cooker – were all waiting and – yes – listening.

Harvey Angell seemed immune to the strange moonlit spell at work in the kitchen. He was too busy setting things up, plugging in the Century Clock and attaching the Energy Charger to a second socket at the back of the

Clock. Immediately the red finger leapt like a frightened bird and the Clock began its slow and fast tick and tock.

'Promising,' said Harvey Angell happily. 'Very promising.' He went over to the piano and opened the lid.

'Now then, Henry,' he said. 'Play!'

'But I *can't* play!' cried Henry. 'I've only ever had one lesson. And this afternoon I picked out a few tunes – but that was when Miss Muggins was here with the *Song Book*. She was singing and I copied her on the piano.'

'That'll do fine,' said Harvey Angell. He picked up the photographs of Aunt Agatha from the top of the piano and examined each of them. 'After all, Henry, you are the great-grandson of the family.'

'But Aunt Agatha will go bonkers if she hears me playing now!' said Henry. Surely, he was thinking, this isn't the kind of thing heroes in adventures are asked to do. They were asked to kill dragons or brave three-headed dogs, not play the piano. Though on reflection, to play the piano was to brave the danger of Aunt Agatha – a feat not unlike daring a dragon. Great and Grand Son, Henry said to himself. And then, to Harvey Angell, 'All right. I'll have a go.'

'Good fellow!' said Harvey Angell.

Henry sat down at the piano and tried to hold his hands as Aunt Agatha had told him. It suddenly seemed important to get things right. He went up and down the stairs of the keyboard, first with his right hand and then with his left. The Century Clock ticked slowly and patiently behind him. Henry tried to play as quietly and as carefully as he could.

Harvey Angell, sitting at the kitchen table, gave a long slow sniff. 'Nothing yet,' he said. 'Not a whiff of anything. Try something else, Henry.'

'I don't know anything else,' said Henry desperately.

'What about the songs you played this afternoon?' asked Harvey Angell. 'You must remember something.'

Henry's mind seemed to have become a total blank as if, once upon a time, it had had writing on it, Useful Things to Know, and now the moonlight, like a large white rubber, had rubbed everything out.

'Think, Henry, think!' pleaded Harvey Angell.

'*God Save the Queen*!' said Henry. 'I think I can remember that.'

Very slowly and very quietly – so that it was almost a piano whisper – Henry picked out the tune of *God Save the Queen* with one finger. At any moment, he thought, Aunt Agatha is going to come storming down the stairs and wither us both with a look.

The Clock ticked normal, steady time.

Harvey Angell gave another long, slow, sniff. 'Still nothing,' he said, disappointedly.

'It's no good,' said Henry, leaving the piano and joining Harvey Angell at the table. 'I'm simply not good enough. What about your flute? I should think Great-Grandma would prefer that.'

'I'm not kin, like you are,' said Harvey Angell. 'But I suppose I could try.'

'I'll sniff,' said Henry helpfully.

'All right,' said Harvey Angell, and he slid the silver flute from its velvet case and stood up.

And then an extraordinary thing happened

that made Henry not simply shiver but turn ice cold with fright.

An invisible hand began picking out a tune on the piano.

Frozen to the spot, Henry watched in horror. How he wished they had stayed in the attic! How he wished he'd never begun this adventure! How he wished for the warm, plump, mostly-earthly Mr Perkins! The Century Clock, like a metronome gone mad, took off with a brisk ticktockticktockticktock. Outside the hollyhocks all rustled together as if trying to raise an alarm.

The invisible piano player was getting into his/her stride now. A second invisible hand joined the first. The tune began to get louder and louder.

'I th-th-thought you said there wouldn't be any gh-gh-ghosts!' stuttered Henry, his teeth chattering. 'Gh-gh-ghosts are against the rules, you said.'

'Well, sometimes the rules do get broken,' said Harvey Angell, quite unperturbed. 'I think we've made it, Henry! Now! Sniff! Sniff!'

Despite himself, Henry sniffed. And slowly the kitchen filled with the sweet, soft smell that was like a summer's apple orchard.

'Lovely as the Garden of Eden,' said Harvey Angell with a sigh.

The scent made Henry feel both dizzy and happy. He felt he was wandering into another world. His whole body now felt as warm and relaxed as if it wasn't the middle of the night in the kitchen at Ballantyre Road, but an afternoon in a garden in mid-July.

And as they both sat there, sniffing and listening and dreaming, Henry suddenly recognised the tune.

'It's *Robin Adair*,' he said. 'The tune – that's what it is.' The words came back to him as if they were written in bright fresh ink on his mind and he sang them, quietly to himself – and to whoever else was in the room.

> Yet him I lov'd so well
> Still in my heart shall dwell.
> Oh! I can ne'er forget
> Robin Adair.

The scent, the warm air, the music now flowing from fluent, invisible fingers, lulled them both into some kind of enchantment.

And the music and the aroma of apple-blossom curled and drifted up out of the kitchen. It drifted up the stairs. It wound its way into every corner of the house. It slid softly under the bedroom doors and into the dreams of all the sleeping occupants of 131 Ballantyre Road.

CHAPTER 16

Mr Perkins, his bed covered in so many pieces of discarded poem that he was like a plump white bird covered in feathers, turned over and smiled in his sleep.

He dreamt he was receiving a prize for the finest book of lyric poems ever written since Shakespeare's Sonnets. He was in a Grand Hall full of Editors who were all cheering him and someone — maybe it was Henry — had put a garland of flowers around his neck. Photographers were flashing flash bulbs at him. Reporters were competing to take down his immortal words in their notebooks. Mr Perkins, in his bed of papers, turned over and sighed contentedly. He thought he could hear music.

Miss Muggins dreamt she was sixteen again and singing in the chapel choir. She was wearing her new dress with sprigs of flowers all over it and a big sash ribbon round the waist and the conductor of the choir was so handsome that Miss Muggins opened her mouth into a sweet, wide O and sang her heart out for the handsome Gwilym Brown who lived over the hill and far away. Miss Muggins sang in her dream and thought she heard someone playing an accompaniment on the piano.

Miss Skivvy, in her powder blue pyjamas, cuddled her pillow and dreamt of a cottage in the country that was all her own and the Head Post Master coming from London to visit her, bringing with him a sack of letters (all with gold stamps) just for her. She snuggled her pillow and thought she smelt the apple-blossom in the garden of her cottage.

Aunt Agatha dreamed of the countryside too. She was out in a meadow with her own little boy and it was a long time ago and they were making a daisy chain together. She put it on his head like a crown. She thought she heard music even though she was in a meadow and it was a sad song and Aunt Agatha cried in her dream and the little boy with the daisy crown vanished and she was suddenly alone and awake. Only now the music was real and her whole bedroom was full of the smell of an orchard and the tune made her cry.

As if they were all sleep-walking, all called by the invisible piano player, Aunt Agatha, Miss Muggins, Miss Skivvy and Mr Perkins got out of their beds and came down to the kitchen.

The piano playing stopped the moment Aunt Agatha opened the kitchen door. Aunt Agatha wore a long, stiff, flannel night-dress that flapped around her ankles as she walked. Her hair was tied up in two bunches that stuck out from her ears like two question marks. Behind her came the dream-walking figures of Mr Perkins (in his red and yellow striped pyjamas), Miss Muggins in a scarlet night shirt with bed socks to match, and Miss Skivvy in her powder blue pyjamas, still hugging her pillow.

Henry shrank against Harvey Angell and waited for his Dragon Aunt to blow fire and wither them both. Harvey Angell put an arm protectively round his shoulders.

But this was a different Aunt Agatha. A dreamy, half-asleep, somehow younger Aunt Agatha, rubbing her eyes and saying, quite gently . . . 'I could have sworn I heard music down here. Someone playing the piano just like Grandma used to do. Was it you, Henry?'

And just as Henry was about to open his mouth and say, 'No, it wasn't me at all, it was a kind of ghost . . . ' Harvey Angell kicked him quite sharply and said, 'Yes, it was, Aunt Agatha. And I'm sorry if we disturbed you.'

To Henry's absolute astonishment, Aunt Agatha said graciously, 'It's quite all right. It was really rather nice. Miss Muggins, put the kettle on, please. Let's have some tea.'

Miss Muggins, pop-eyed with surprise, hurried to obey. 'I thought I heard it, too,' she said. 'And it was a song I know quite well – it's on the tip of my tongue, if only I could remember it.'

'It was *Robin*,' said Aunt Agatha, so gently that

for a moment Henry could almost believe that Aunt Agatha had the tender soul Mr Perkins thought she had. '*Robin Adair*,' she continued. 'It reminded me of my own dear Robin and I was dreaming of the day he and I went out into the country and made daisy chains. But that's all I can remember.'

Mr Perkins, without asking anyone, produced a tin of biscuits. Miss Muggins poured tea. Miss Skivvy sat down and rocked herself as if she was still dreaming of her country cottage and the sack of golden stamped letters brought by the Head Post Master.

'Robin? Who's Robin?' asked Henry.

'Why, that's Robin, of course,' said Aunt Agatha, pointing to the photograph of herself and the baby. Mr Perkins took the photograph from the top of the piano and handed it to her. Henry came and stood by his Aunt.

'He was only four when he died,' said Aunt Agatha. 'He died three years before your parents died in that awful car crash. Robin had leukaemia. It meant he lost all his hair. You'd have liked him, Henry, you really would.'

'I'm sure I would,' said Henry. He found it very hard to swallow his biscuit. So that, he was thinking, was the second sorrow. The second sorrow, the source of the sorrow which Aunt Agatha had refused to speak about and which had withered and gnarled her and made the house cold and unhappy. And the daisies! Why the daisy smell in the attic must have been the essence of Robin.

'Did Robin sleep in the attic?' he asked.

'Why, yes, he did, dear,' said Aunt Agatha, sipping her tea.

('Dear', thought Henry! She called me 'dear'!)

'Your mother hoped that one day she would move from Scotland and come and live nearby – then you and Robin would grow up together, like brothers,' said Aunt Agatha. 'But it wasn't to be.'

And now Henry saw two tears drop onto the photograph of the young Aunt Agatha and baby Robin.

'There! There, dear! Don't take on so,' said Miss Muggins, hurrying to put an arm round

Aunt Agatha's bony shoulders. But Harvey Angell waved her away.

'It's all right,' he said. 'Crying is good for people sometimes.'

So Aunt Agatha had a very good cry and Mr Perkins found her a large clean duster to blow her nose on and Miss Muggins made some more, stronger, tea. Miss Skivvy seemed to come round from her dream. She stopped rocking and cuddling her cushion and said, 'I'd like some more music now,' just as if she was ordering hot chocolate and toast at the Waifs and Strays Café.

I suppose, thought Henry, looking around him, we're all waifs and strays of one kind or another.

'There's such a sweet smell in here,' said Miss Skivvy. 'It reminds me of when I was a girl in the country.'

The apple-blossom smell had faded with the music but something of it still lingered in the kitchen.

'Is this a breakthrough?' Henry whispered to Harvey Angell.

'What do you think?' Harvey Angell whispered back.

Henry nodded.

'I think some more music is a very good idea,' said Harvey Angell.

'Ladies and Gentlemen,' said Henry. 'I think you should all know that Harvey Angell . . . ' But this time he received an even sharper kick.

'No need for explanations, Henry,' said Harvey Angell. 'Some things are much better left to music,' and he gave Henry the Full Beam.

'I would like some more music too,' declared Aunt Agatha. 'But first, there is something I would like to show to Henry. Mr Perkins, perhaps you'd fetch the painting from Henry's room for me.'

Mr Perkins bustled off and was back in the tick of a Century's Clock.

When he returned, everyone crowded round to look at the painting.

'Now look in this corner,' said Aunt Agatha. 'Can you see initials there?'

Henry peered at the right hand corner of the painting. He had looked at it every night without seeing them before. 'Yes. Yes, I can,' he said. 'E.E.'

'And?' prompted Aunt Agatha.

'E.E.' repeated Henry. 'Why – Elizabeth Entwistle. My mother painted it!'

'She did indeed,' said Aunt Agatha. 'She was the true artist of the family and your great-grandma and I were the musicians. Do you recognise the house, Henry?' she asked.

'I've always thought it looked the most homely house ever,' said Henry. 'That's why I liked the painting.'

'It's hard to see the house properly,' said Miss Muggins, 'because of the glow of light coming from the hall. It's a very welcoming light – but it hides the house.'

'Look very carefully,' said Aunt Agatha. 'Look at the window on the left and those flowers rather low down.'

'I've got it!' cried Mr Perkins at exactly the same moment as Henry cried, 'Hollyhocks!'

'It's this house!' said Miss Skivvy. 'Well I never.'

'Lizzie painted it when she was about sixteen,'

said Aunt Agatha. 'That's a long time ago. The hollyhocks were very low then. It was Lizzie who planted them.'

'I always thought that was the house I would like to live in,' said Henry. 'The house that was *really* home.'

'And you were living in it all the time!' said Harvey Angell. 'Well, watts and volts. There's a thunderbolt. I mean – a big surprise!'

Mr Perkins seemed quite overcome by all the excitement and surprises. 'I should like to read you my poem,' he said.

'What a good idea,' said Harvey Angell. 'A poem is just what we all need to re-charge our batteries. A poem is the liquid fluid that connects us all.'

'Blake,' said Henry.

'Wrong!' said Harvey Angell. 'Harvey Angell.'

'Oh my, Mr Angell is quite poetical too,' said Miss Muggins.

'Up on the table with you,' cried Harvey Angell to Mr Perkins. And Mr Perkins, looking rather flushed but very important, clambered up onto the table (a thing Henry never, ever, imagined possible at 131 Ballantyre Road) and produced his poem from the pocket of his pyjama jacket.

Turning to Aunt Agatha, he began:

Dear Agatha, my dear, my dove,
Dear Agatha, please be my love.
My heart is like your piano keys,
I hear sonatas when you sneeze.
I'd give up cake and jam for tea,
If only you would marry me.

Everyone applauded and it was Aunt Agatha's turn to blush.

'What happened to "boiled potatoes, peas and ham"?' asked Henry, who had been looking forward to that bit.

'I cut them out,' said Mr Perkins.

Miss Muggins and Miss Skivvy were all in a flutter waiting to hear Aunt Agatha's answer.

'My dear Mr Perkins,' said Aunt Agatha. 'It is most kind of you to ask, but I think we must put Art before Love, don't you agree?'

('A little unrequited love is good for poets,' Aunt Agatha whispered to Harvey Angell.)

Mr Perkins sighed deeply and said yes, he supposed she was right. And Miss Muggins and Miss Skivvy sighed deeply too and said nothing because secretly they didn't think too much of Art.

'And now it really is time for a sing-song,' said Harvey Angell. 'Aunt Agatha, it's your turn to play the piano!'

Very happily Aunt Agatha took her place at the piano and played every tune she could remember, including *Robin Adair* – only it didn't sound so sad when everyone sang it together. And when she played Polly-Wolly-Doodle, Miss Muggins, Miss Skivvy and Mr Perkins all linked arms and danced around the kitchen.

'Here's to pianos that are never locked!' cried Mr Perkins, waving his tea mug in the air.

'Here's to hearts and pianos that are always open!' sang Miss Muggins.

None of them noticed Harvey Angell leaving or saw the hollyhocks shaking their heads as he went off down Ballantyre Road in the darkness, his canvas tool bag slung over his back.

It was only when Miss Muggins had fallen

asleep with her head on the kitchen table and Mr Perkins had sung himself hoarse, that they looked round and saw that he'd gone.

'Perhaps he's gone to bed,' said Henry. 'After all, he's had a very busy day. I'll go up and see.'

Feeling very tired himself, Henry went up to the attic. But the attic was bare. Harvey Angell had left the window wide open and a message on the bed for Henry.

It said, 'Remember me, your friend Harvey Angell, as I shall remember you. This isn't really goodbye. I shall see you on the Circuit.'

Henry was so tired that he climbed into the bed that had been Harvey Angell's and fell fast asleep.

Aunt Agatha found him there a little while later and tucked him in. 'Henry might as well have the attic now,' she said to Mr Perkins.

'Yes,' said Mr Perkins. 'It's a good room for a boy. Do you know, I can't find the key to the piano anywhere. I think Harvey Angell must have taken it.'

'Ah well,' said Aunt Agatha, 'we won't be needing it.'

In the morning, none of them could remember the night before.

'Funny, Mr Angell just vanishing like that,' said Miss Muggins.

'Yes,' said Miss Skivvy, 'and the white hollyhocks have vanished too.'

'He's left us enough,' said Aunt Agatha.

Turn over to read the first chapter
of Henry and Harvey Angell's
next adventure,
Harvey Angell and the Ghost Child!

CHAPTER 1

Henry was worried about his Aunt Agatha. She was not her old mean and miserable self. It was true she still counted her tea bags at night and no one could say that the portion of potatoes she spooned out at supper time to Henry, Mr Perkins, Miss Muggins and Miss Skivvy was exactly generous, but for all that, Aunt Agatha was a changed woman.

Aunt Agatha was happy! Trillingly, smilingly, chillingly happy! A rainy day, awful news, a terrible cold – nothing seemed to dim Aunt Agatha's happiness. It was curiously bothersome, as though Aunt Agatha had lost her weather, had no spring, summer, autumn and winter any more, only one long and constant smiley summer.

It was not that Henry wanted the old Aunt Agatha back – Aunt Agatha of the wintery withers, Aunt Agatha who kept both her piano and her heart tightly locked and whose sorrow had filled 131 Ballantyre Road with a dusty grey gloom; Aunt Agatha as she had been before the arrival of Harvey Angell. No, Henry certainly didn't want *that* Aunt Agatha back.

Harvey Angell had changed not just Aunt Agatha but the whole house. He had changed 131 Ballantyre Road from a House of Sorrow to a House of Happiness.

'Watts and volts, watts and volts, better by far than thunderbolts,' Henry often sang to himself when he remembered how for one brief week in the summer Harvey Angell had come to live in the attic. What strange gear he had pulled out of his electrician's tool bag on that first morning! A bundle of screwdrivers with brightly coloured handles – well, they'd been ordinary enough – but after them came what Harvey Angell called his Connecting Kit, his Energy Charger and the magical Centuries Clock.

At first Henry had thought that Harvey Angell was up to no good, sniffing about the house as he did, going off to graveyards and playing his silver flute. It made Henry grin to think how he and Mr Perkins had played detectives, following Harvey Angell through the city streets and ending up at the amazing Waifs and Strays Café.

It was there, over a Supernova burger, that Henry had learnt about Harvey Angell's strange profession of 'Homer'. It was a job, Henry thought, that was something like an electrician's and rather more like a *mag*ician's.

'What I do,' Harvey Angell had said, cheerfully tucking in to Earthly Bangers and Mash, 'is connect the living and the dead. We're all on the same circuit, you see.' (That was the electrics.) 'Only people forget that. They switch off, like you switch off an electric light!' Sorrow, Harvey Angell had explained, made people switch off and the Energy – the energy that was a kind of love – was switched off too. What Harvey Angell did, what all Homers did, was connect people up to the Energy Supply. And that was the magic. And that was what he'd done at 131 Ballantyre Road. He'd released Aunt

Agatha's sorrow. He'd switched them all on again. He'd connected them to the Energy.

But, Henry thought, was it possible that a little too much Energy had got into the circuit and that Aunt Agatha – and Mr Perkins too, for that matter – had somehow been super-charged?

Henry remembered how Mr Perkins, quiet and sober Mr Perkins, had danced about in the graveyard in his pyjamas, declaring himself divinely sparked and thinking this was a huge joke. A 'spark', Mr Perkins had said, was the slang word for an electrician and now he, Mr Perkins, had been divinely sparked – and he'd gone off to the park to write a soppy love poem about Aunt Agatha. Mr Perkins was deep in unrequited love for Aunt Agatha and Aunt Agatha said this was good for him (as if love was like spinach or vitamin pills) because it sharpened his verse.

And now, in his super-charged state, Mr Perkins had bought himself half a dozen pairs of pyjamas and appeared regularly in the park as a Performance Poet. He'd taken to clicking his fingers between lines and pushing back his few remaining wisps of hair and flinging his arms about. It was all extremely embarrassing to Henry.

And Aunt Agatha, in her extra-happy state, was no better. Aunt Agatha had taken to pushing the piano out into the street every Friday morning and busking there, much to the amusement of the boys at school who wanted to know if Aunt Agatha was planning to go on *Britain's Got Talent* and if everyone in Henry's house was a nutter – including Henry.

'Henry Oddity' they called him and they had a rhyme they sang. They sang it in the playground. Sometimes, walking home from school, a trio of girls would sing it behind his back:

> Henry Oddity
> What a clod is he
> A curiosity
> Henry Oddity.

Henry hated it. He badly wanted to be just like everyone else. And even more badly he wanted a friend. It wasn't just the goings-on of Aunt Agatha and Mr Perkins that made the others nickname him Henry Oddity and left him feeling lonely, clumsy and cloddish, it was the clothes!

Aunt Agatha bought him jumble-sale clothes. Henry didn't mind the oldness of the clothes – indeed, he thought old clothes were much more comfortable than new ones. But Aunt Agatha never took Henry with her when she went jumbling (as she called it) and as a result nothing fitted properly. Henry had trousers that were too short, too long, too baggy or too tight and jerseys that looked as if they'd been knitted by someone who was colour blind. Henry must have been the only boy in school (apart from Jed Lomax who was another friendless oddity) who didn't have a pair of trainers. When Henry looked at himself in the mirror he didn't notice his warm brown eyes or his friendly smile. He only saw what he thought the others saw – an oddity.

To make matters worse, in her happy state, Aunt Agatha's 'jumbling' grew wilder. Proudly she brought home T-shirts and jerseys in such bright, clashing colours that even Mrs Towers (Henry's class teacher) said, 'My word, Henry, I need sunglasses to look at you this morning!'

The car which Aunt Agatha bought might

also have come from a jumble sale. It was a very old, very cheap, rattly Rover. Happiness had not cured Aunt Agatha of her skinflint ways, but it had cured her of greyness. She sprayed the car bright pink and drove it in much the same way as she played the piano – her foot on the loud pedal/ accelerator. And for extra cheer, the pink Rover was fitted with a special horn that played the first three notes of Beethoven's Fifth Symphony because, said Aunt Agatha, she wanted to make sure that people knew she was coming. And everyone certainly did!

'Jenson Button rides again,' said the boys when now and again Aunt Agatha, wearing teddy-bear ear muffs, took it into her head to collect Henry (whose own ears burnt bright red with embarrassment) from school.

And as if Henry didn't have enough to cope with, even Miss Muggins and Miss Skivvy – who before Harvey Angell's visit had been two shy and timid old dears – were no longer either. Miss Muggins had joined the town's operatic society and was currently rehearsing, mostly when Henry was trying to sleep, for 'HMS *Pinafore*'. As for Miss Skivvy, who'd worked in the post office for so many years that she'd come to look like a brown paper parcel herself, well, Miss Skivvy had retired and begun doing a sandwich round for the homeless – on a skateboard.

She made excuses about the skateboard, of course. Said her legs were poorly and skateboarding helped her get about. Even though Henry admired Miss Skivvy no end – and sometimes helped her make the sandwiches – it didn't help his image when she whizzed past the school gates at lunch time and the boys called out, 'Hey! There goes Skivvy-Saintboard!'

It was just when Henry was wondering if the Energy level in the house might run down just a little and make life more normal that he came downstairs for breakfast to find Aunt Agatha and Mr Perkins dancing.

Mr Perkins was shaking the tin he used in the park to collect money. Aunt Agatha was shaking the tin she used when busking on her piano, and together they made a terrific noise. They shook their tins like maracas, and Aunt Agatha tossed her skirts, and Mr Perkins clicked his fingers high in the air and stamped his feet, and Henry had a very hard job making himself heard.

'What's going on?' asked Henry. 'Have we won the lottery?'

'No!' cried Aunt Agatha, doing a twirl. 'But we've made enough money to go on holiday! We're going to the seaside, Henry!'

Then Henry's heart lurched because for all the years since his parents had died and he'd lived with Aunt Agatha, he'd never been on holiday. And he'd never seen the sea.

Henry's own energy level shot up like the mercury in a thermometer, like a kettle brought to the boil, like a battery recharged. Super-charged!

'The seaside!' cried Henry and he and Mr Perkins and Aunt Agatha linked arms and danced round the kitchen table.

And in the weeks that followed, super-charged – or sea-charged – was how everyone in 131 Ballantyre Road stayed. Miss Skivvy bought herself a straw hat, a striped swimming costume and a pair of orange armbands which she wore at supper time. ('Just to get used to them.') Miss Muggins sang sea-shanties – 'What Shall we Do with the Drunken Sailor' and 'The Big Ship Sails through the Alley Alley O' being her favourites. Mr Perkins recited 'The Seafarer', which Henry thought was a very miserable poem as the seafarer always seemed very cold. He had icicles in his beard and was missing someone. Mr Perkins also read them a list of names for the sea which he'd found in a book called the *Odyssey*. There was the 'fish-haunted deep' and the 'darkling ripple'; the 'Salty Abyss', 'Ocean's Pouring Stream' and 'The Briny Water' and many more.

Sometimes Henry lay in the bath practising his back stroke and murmuring 'the boundless sea' and 'the waveworn caves', for the rhythm of these made him feel as if he was in a boat. Afterwards he'd sail a few sponges in the bath water and pretend it was the 'fish-quick sea'. Dreaming of the sea was a kind of escape from loneliness.

Aunt Agatha had a different way of dreaming about the seaside. She spent her evenings counting the money in the busking tins and doing what she called her Holiday Budget. There was no budging Aunt Agatha from her budget. She wrote down everything she could think of that they might possibly spend money on.

'Put down fish and chips,' said Mr Perkins.

'And ice cream,' said Miss Muggins.

'And candyfloss and rock,' said Miss Skivvy. 'And perhaps a donkey ride.'

Aunt Agatha put down her pencil. 'I don't think it's that kind of seaside,' she said. But when they asked her what kind of seaside it was, she wouldn't tell them. It was to be a surprise.

Night after night, Aunt Agatha, Mr Perkins, Miss Muggins and Miss Skivvy talked of seasides they had known. The lights and the big dipper at Blackpool (Miss Muggins); a little Cornish cove (Miss Skivvy); the pier at New Brighton (Mr Perkins); Sea View Guest House on the Gower (Aunt Agatha). Only Henry said nothing. Henry had his own picture of the seaside in his head, a picture that seemed almost too precious to share.

There would be miles and miles of sand, of course. And rocks to clamber about. There would be shining, shimmery, tossing blue waves to dash in and out of. There would be ice cream three times a day and little boats bobbing in the distance and permanent sunshine. And most importantly, your eyes wouldn't be cut short, as they were in the city, by big buildings and huge walls. There'd be 'boundless sea' and 'waveworn caves'. In one of these, Henry imagined, there still might linger an occasional smuggler or pirate. And if there weren't smugglers or pirates there would certainly be an adventure of some sort or another.

And that was one of the few things Henry was right about.